# Gift of Change

# Gift of Change

D Sanders

Writer's Showcase
San Jose New York Lincoln Shanghai

**Gift of Change**



Writer's Showcase
an imprint of iUniverse.com, Inc.

For information address:
iUniverse.com, Inc.
5220 S 16th, Ste. 200
Lincoln, NE 68512
www.iuniverse.com

ISBN: 0-595-19326-9

Printed in the United States of America

# I

"General quarters! General quarters! All hands to your battle stations," blasted out of the engineering plant's main control speakers.

Jason McCullan, Lieutenant Commander of the Imperial Navy and Chief Engineer of the Crusher class deep space cruiser, Shing-Twa, watched as his finely tuned crew rushed to their stations. He knew their hearts were pounding because this wasn't a drill and they all knew it.

"Number 2 engineering control station on line and fully staffed," a hard faced Lieutenant reported from a holographic miniature control station on Jason's console. All the engineering control stations reported, staffed and ready, within twenty seconds. After a quick look at his own console, Jason announced to the computer, "Bridge, Main control, all engineering spaces staffed and ready. We await your convenience Commodore." The image of a steely eyed, salt and peppered bristled haired, tyrant appeared on the top center of Jason's console. It was the captain of the Shing-Twa and squadron commander of strike force 143, Commodore Hansen. Jason knew there was an image of himself standing on the bridge at the chief engineer post.

"Mr. McCullan, make alterations to the main cannons and preparations to shoot. Let me know when you are ready," the Commodore didn't even look at him.

Jason was confused. He didn't remember any alterations. As a matter of fact, he couldn't remember much of anything about the engineering plant or systems on the Shing-Twa.

"Mr. McCullan, you look confused. Is there a problem?" There wasn't a hint of compassion the Commodore's voice.

"Ah, Alteration? I don't remember any alterations."

"This was your plan! You were the one that assured me the main guns' range and power could be increased by ten." The Commodore stood with his hands behind his back.

"Commodore, I don't remember why we were altering the cannons." Jason was starting to feel real uncomfortable. He seemed to remember having done all this before, but not like this.

"By the blazing sun, McCullan! How could you forget that we are outnumbered ten to one and outgunned by closer to twenty? I just ordered the rebels to stand down or be destroyed to a being, upon your recommendation. "

Jason was sweating hard now. He could almost remember. He had done this all before. "Commodore, is this a deep space emergency?"

"Yes, by god, I'd say it is or it will be, when I march down there to personally shoot you."

Jason's mind cleared and knowledge seemed to pour in. He remembered all the weapon systems alterations, the plan he had proposed to the Commodore, and every other system and power grid on the Shing-Twa. "Not a problem Commodore, give me ten minutes, then bring the squadron about." He didn't wait for the Commodore's reply. Jason's hands started flashing over the instrument panel. This was how he remembered it going.

"Weapon control stations one through six, stand by for configuration download." He pulled up from engcomp memory the reconfiguration programming and schematics for the physical changes needed. He sent the data on to the weapon control stations.

Someone was screaming at him. He looked up to see the ship's PsySec officer walking toward him. The man's mouth moved, but Jason heard an alarm wail instead of words.

Jason was furious. PsySec officers were arrogant and overbearing with over inflated egos. Ordinarily, Jason would have had to tolerate his presence, but not at battle stations. "We're at battle stations, mister! Clear my spaces." Jason turned his attention back to his instrument and sensor read outs.

He watched as the weapons' technicians altered the helistic lens, the graviton fields, and pulse chambers to allow nuclear fusion to continue the length of the cannon barrel. It would be equivalent to increasing the energy compression chamber by four times on each axis or total volume by 56 times, thus increasing range and intensity by well over 10 times. Unfortunately, it would also burn out the cannon after only ten or so shots. It was a waste, since the cannons were designed to last the life of the ship, but it was a tradeoff the Commodore was willing to make. They were in a bad situation. A squadron of one heavy cruiser, five destroyers, four frigates, and seven corvettes against a rebel fleet of two in system battleships, five in system cruisers, twelve destroyers, and thirty corvettes, frigates, and gunboats.

A hand closed on his arm and shook him. Startled, Jason looked into the face of a PsySec officer he almost recognized. "You've been Civ..." the PsySec guy started to say, but got cut off by a wailing noise that made Jason's head hurt.

Jason pushed him away, "Get out of my spaces! We are at battle stations. I don't have time for your complaints." Jason turned back to his console. All weapons' stations were showing green and ready for shooting orders. "Bridge, Main control. We are ready Commodore."

"Good job, Mr. McCullan. My compliments to your engineering staff. Make preparations for full power operations. Bring all plasma fields on line, standby for damage control." The Commodore's holograph looked off at something Jason couldn't see. "Orders to the squadron." The Commodore paused, "Come left to formation Q17. Launch all fighters." He was maneuvering the other ships into formation.

Jason mentally reviewed all the engineering systems on the Shing-Twa highlighting in his mind the potential trouble areas. He had virtually rebuilt the power grid on the ship, not to mention the entire engineering department, since becoming the Chief Engineer. He knew every system like the back of his hand. "Number three engineering control station dispatch a damage control team to gravity control node three." Jason continued to preposition damage control teams at the weak spots he envisioned.

"Send to the rebel fleet," the commodore paused to let the communications office make the connection, "Surrender now and no lives will be lost." Jason couldn't hear the response, but the Commodore's face became like stone. "Then die in the cold of space." He made a quick motion with his hand, severing the connection. "Mr. Conner, target the preselected ships. Full speed ahead. Take them as they come within range, Mr. Conner."

The weapons officer, Mr. Conner, wasn't on Jason's com circuit, but Jason watched the ion torroids, the fusion generators powering the weapons, come online one at a time. Then the ship jerked, overload lights began flashing, and the temperature dropped in the plasma field of one ion torroid. They had fired the cannon.

Before Jason could issue an order, his damage control teams had leaped into action. Almost as fast as the lights went red, they would flicker back to green. He was proud of his men and women.

A hand landed on his shoulder and spun Jason around. The PsySec officer was standing there, "This is a dream. You can't remember this information. Please forget it all. You've been Civ..." The wailing started again giving Jason a head and stomachache. He pushed the officer away.

The ship lurched several times and more lights appeared. Jason's engineering staff was smoothly handling all the overloads and burnouts. He had trained them well. "Is this a dream?" he asked himself. It was so real. He felt proud of his engineering team.

"Mr. McCullan," the Commodore commanded his attention, "You are a bloody, nova genius. We've gutted both battleships and taken out most of the cruisers. The enemy isn't even close to their maximum gun range yet. I'll see your decorated and promoted. Pass on to your people to keep up the good work."

"Thank you, Commodore." Guilt washed over Jason. He had been decorated and promoted. This was a dream. He was just reliving the glory.

The PsySec officer, Mr. Guildron, who had Civilized Jason when he retired his commission, stepped in front of him. "Mr. McCullan this is forbidden. You have been Civilized. This knowledge is classified. You must forget it."

Jason's stomach rebelled, "No! I don't want to forget. I don't want to be Civilized." In one fluid motion, he drew his sidearm and shot Mr. Guildron between the eyes.

# II

Jason woke up sitting in front of the navigation panel on his deep space freighter, Boundless, doubled over, dry retching onto the floor, and crying.

A wailing scream rang through the bridge.

"Shut Up! CAN'T YOU BE QUIET!" Jason screamed as he slammed his hand down on the intercom cutout. Silence descended on the bridge as he pulled himself together after another nightmare.

"Jason, my sensors detected no noise on the bridge, other than the ones you were making," the soft voice of his ship's computer informed him.

Not hearing, Jason leaned his head wearily against the console and muttered, "What did I ever do to deserve this? I did my twenty-five years with the Imperial Navy, got decorated, won top honors, and retired. Got Civilized," a pang of guilt shot through him as he thought of how unfair it had been for them to make him forget the classified military secrets he had lived with for twenty-five years. Guilt was the method used by the Civilization process for keeping aggressively minded people within societal norms. Any time he thought against the Imperial government, societal rules, or desired to do physical harm to anyone, guilt would literally make him sick and dizzy. "It's fair," he said to no one, "they couldn't have me running around with all those aggressive behaviors." The nausea subsided. He breathed a sigh of relief.

He was eighteen days out on a simple cargo run from Delter to Plet, a couple of backwater systems. Jason was tired. The Boundless, originally designed for a crew of fourteen, had been automated and modified by Jason so that three could run it. Jason had fired the mate because the man was caught stealing and his pilot partner was in jail on Delter. Running things alone was going to stretch him thin, but he'd done it before. Then, on the second day the nightmares started. He was reliving all the worst parts of his life, or at least parts he wasn't supposed to remember, while he slept. These events seemed to be the very things the Civilization process didn't like. He woke violently ill several times a night. A man does not function well on three hours of sleep a day and being unable to hold down meals.

He shifted his position slightly, pillowed his head a little more, and his elbow landed on several switches. "Damn you, Falon for getting this blasted cargo." He whined, "And damn you for getting thrown in the brig. Why did you pick this time to get into a fight over honor? You never cared before. And of all people to get into a fight with, why did you have to do it with the law enforcers?" Shifting his position his mumbling got softer. "Of all times, why this time, on a forty day run? You know that I'm not the best pilot anymore. Remember, I fix it, you fly it." The mumbling stopped as he went to sleep.

# III

Jason looked up to see a blinking yellow light and a red warning banner flashing on all the monitors and holonav. He shook his head, rubbed his gritty eyes, and then he heard a soft chime. Still groggy, he groped around until he found the right switches. Flipping the switches, the bridge erupted with the noise of a raging klaxon and a screaming siren. The deck vibrated with the intensity of the sound. After a few seconds of total disorientation and wild clawing, Jason found the same switches and threw them again. The gentle chiming returned.

He was wide-awake now. His head was pounding, but he didn't feel sick. With strange alternating feelings of dread and elation, Jason began tracing the reason for the alarms. He brought up the maintenance and test displays to query the engineering computers. All systems were reporting massive failures and overrides. Every emergency system had been initiated in some form or another. Moving unsteadily across the deck, Jason arrived at the manual override panel, quickly removed the protection cover and flipped four override switches. A different kind of life returned to the bridge as panels blinked and displays shifted screens and data. He had brought the central computer core back on-line. "Fred, what's going on?"

A soft, evenly modulated, slightly feminine voice answered, "You'll have to be more specific Jason. I'm only a level two system."

"Okay. Okay. Why are the energizers shut down? Why are all the emergency systems active?"

"The energizers aren't working properly. All systems suffered cascading failures."

"I know all that! Don't you start on that verbatim compliance crap again. Now tell me why?"

"Jason you know I'm only a level two system and my independent reasoning capabilities are limited by my AI programming."

"Knock off that inferiority crap. You're the best we could afford. Tell me why the energizers are shut down."

The voice lost some of its feminine quality and gained a lot of bluntness, "There is an abnormality in the number two mass exchanger that is causing a high fluctuation in the ion stream of number two engine."

"What caused the abnormality?"

"I'm not sure. I'm not human. I'm only a..."

Jason was able to interrupt, only because he had programmed it to stop talking when he spoke, "I know. I know." His voice rose in pitch as he mimicked the computer, "I am only a limit two artificial semi-intelligent unit with reduced core capacity." He threw his hands in the air, "Why did I ever update you?"

"Because Scott and Fulton quit and you had to automate the ship."

"Thanks a lot Fred. I had almost forgotten."

"You asked the question I was only answering it, as I am programmed to do."

"Fred."

"Yes, Jason."

"Shut up." An audible snap came through the speakers followed by a slight power hum. "Fred knock off the power hum or I'll short the core again." The hum went away.

Jason quickly scanned several areas trying to pinpoint the trouble. Getting confusing answers, he decided to find out his ship's location. Piloting was not his main talent, but celestial navigation is just an extension of geometry, so it shouldn't be hard. Jason brought up the nav screens, identified the closest stars, and then struggled for ten minutes trying to triangulate the fix. Throwing down the stylus in frustration Jason exploded, "Why did they block navigation? How could any idiot ever have figured that it was vital military knowledge." Jason instantly got dizzy and nauseated. "I can calculate the mass flow density needed to reach .1 light speed using a four engine ion stream in my head, but I can't figure out where we are in space. This isn't fair." Jason whined. After a few moments of self pity and several deep drinks from the squeeze bottle he carried, Jason asked, "Fred, where are we?" The holonav expanded to its typical configuration and filled with the image of stars and space. Against an extensive asteroid reef, a red dot appeared. "Thanks," Jason breathed out.

"Jason," Fred quietly intoned, "the ship is broken. Would you please fix it. It might blow up if something isn't done."

Jason jerked as if shocked. "That's right it is. I...I...I can still fix things." He leaped up and quickly moved back to the maintenance console.

"Jason you are not acting normal. You are acting more depressed than normal. You should report to the med unit."

Jason wasn't listening. Any time he started working on a problem, he went into his own world. It was the only thing left untouched by the Civilization process or at least it seemed that way. He was still very good at it.

Jason worked feverishly for several minutes then sat back to watch the preprogrammed diagnostics and visual scans.

"Ah, Fred, ah...number ten scan isn't working."

"Yes it is Jason."

"What do you mean, yes it is? If it was working, then I'd be able to see number two cable bundle and number two mass feed line."

"That is true, Jason. You would also be able to see the cargo, which is prohibited under article fourteen of the contract of shipment."

"Knock off the crap and clear the linkage."

"I can't do that Jason. It would breach the contract and cost you money. You were the one that set up the maximized cost benefit analysis program."

"There must be some clause that will allow me to view the cargo for the safety of the ship. Fred, we've been arguing about this since we lifted ship, eighteen days now. I think it's time you found a way around the contract."

"It's been nineteen days."

"It's been nineteen days what?"

"It's been nineteen days that we've been arguing about the contract."

"Fred don't start getting weird on me. We both know that it's...it's...ah Fred...ah...how long was I a sleep?"

"Sixteen hours, seventeen minutes, sixteen seconds."

"SIXTEEN HOURS!!!" Jason's mind began conjuring up all the things that could happen to a ship traveling just over .3 the speed of light without a pilot. He shook himself, counted to ten, and in what he thought was an even tone, yelled, "WHY DIDN'T YOU WAKE ME?"

"You had shut down the speech centers of my core. It was just a few hours into your nap that the problem occurred," the computer announced in an irritatingly smooth tone.

Jason sat stiff-backed, grasping the arms of the chair. His face was a picture of pure horror. "I'm lucky to be alive. No pilot for sixteen hours in an asteroid reef, how did I survive?"

Fred answered barely audible, "I managed to alter course twice and get the shields up once."

Jason was shocked out of his deep funk. "You did what? Say that again. I want to be sure I heard you right."

"I managed to alter course twice and get the shields up once."

This was one shock too many. He took it in stride, "I didn't know you could do that. How did you do that?"

"In all honesty I didn't know I could either, but with the ship bearing down on a particularly large asteroid I began trying anything I could think of."

Jason cocked his head, "Think of?"

"Well, I am semi-intelligent and I do have a learning algorithm, not a very good one, but I do have one."

"You don't even have flight centers programmed in. What did you use for a basis of the algorithm?"

"Falon has a wide selection of flight simulator programs that are used to test reflex action and visual skill. I have to play her adversaries. All of the sessions are recorded for play back. I studied them and learned the basics."

Jason was impressed. He had made a few alterations in the hardware, software and photonic interfaces, not quite according to the manual, but still. He lost himself for a few minutes trying to figure out what he had actually done. Shaking his head he asked, "But that still doesn't answer the question of how you actually maneuvered the ship. You don't have any overrides for the main controls. Fred how did you turn the ship?"

"You're not going to like it."

"I already don't like it. Answer my question."

"I altered the mass flow rates to the engines and used the differential thrust to turn the ship."

Jason groaned, "And let me guess. You used the energizers as the throttling mechanism?" There was a long silence. "Well was that what you did?"

"You said that you wanted to guess."

"Don't get cute."

"Okay, that was almost how I did it."

"And that was when the abnormality in the energizer began. What do you mean almost?"

"Are you still guessing?"

"NO! I'm not still guessing. Now, DAMN IT, tell me what happened."

"I changed course using the energizers to control fuel flow rate to the ion fusion chambers and further controlled the thrust rate by varying the gravatonic field in the ion lens. Both energizers did experience a slight fluctuation but steadied out after each use. Sensors showed no change in the ion lens function. Then an asteroid with a large delta vee resolved itself from the surroundings with a constant bearing and decreasing range. The delta vee was too great for the navigation method described. I overrode the shield relay to energize the shields, calculating that it would deflect the asteroid. The asteroid struck us amidships starboard and that was when the energizers shut down and all systems cascaded to fail safe."

Jason turned pale as he considered the implications. He was still breathing so some of the systems worked correctly. "Was the shield relay destroyed when you overrode the locking signal?"

"I'm afraid so Jason."

"Damn! Do you know how much a Fletcher relay costs and how many hours it takes to replace one?"

"Do you want the figures?"

"No. I don't want the figures. What happened next?"

"We drifted. I was knocked off line. You woke up."

"Great." Jason sat whining, drinking, and muttering to himself while mulling over the situation. Finally, deciding he had to do something, he brought all the internal diagnostics on-line and began a comprehensive ship system scan. It was quite possible that the ship suffered massive system damage with shields activated just before a catastrophic collision took place. Shield failures could be very nasty, not to mention getting hit by a rock. Shields would only stop a mass up to a certain point and small energy weapons. He had modified the shields using a different technology than originally designed, which should have increased their capabilities by about a thousand times. But, would it have held against an asteroid impact, Jason wondered? With the diagnostics running, Jason began reviewing the onboard spares and salvage equipment available.

Jason's life after Imperial naval service was this ship. He spent all his time and money on repairing, updating, and modifying just about every system on the ship. His career had been as a researcher, an engineering officer in a fleet yard, then finally as the chief engineer on a Star Destroyer class cruiser. There wasn't anything he couldn't fix given time and the necessary parts. In some cases, he didn't need the parts. One of his big investments had been a semi-portable manufacturing center, that given the dimensions and raw material, it would turn out the part in just a few hours.

While the diagnostics ran, Jason began to calculate how far off course they were, but after fifteen minutes of sheer frustration whined, "Fred how far off course are we?"

"I've been wondering when you were going to ask me. I'm sorry Jason if I did the wrong thing."

"No, you did the right thing. It's just that you shouldn't have been able to do what you did and that scares me a little. How far off course are we?"

A glowing violet dot appeared in the holonav connected to the red dot by a green line, "Four days."

Jason looked at it in mute silence. With a heavy sigh, he fell back in his chair. "Four days," he whined. "How much catalyst did we lose?"

"About ninety three percent of the energizer catalyst."

"That's it. I'm dead." Jason collapsed with his head down on the console slowly rocking back and forth.

"Why don't you get some sleep Jason? You will feel better after some sleep and food." Fred offered in his best soothing voice.

"Okay Fred, I'll go to sleep for a while." He paused for a moment as some life returned to him. "I want you to do two things; first compute the distance and time to the nearest hyperspace jump point, and second find a flaw in that contract so that I can go into the hold to do repairs." He started off the bridge, "Also, for your own information, shields won't stop big asteroids."

"I know that now."

The Captain's underway cabin was adjoining the bridge, so he didn't have to go far. Clearing dirty clothes and empty whisky squeeze dispensers off the bed he called out, "I'm going to leave the intercom open. Wake me when the diagnostics are done." Jason was asleep before his head touched the pillow.

# IV

Jason woke in a cold sweat. He had been having a dream about being chased around a cage by a hideous monster that kept talking to him in a language he didn't understand. The conversation faded when he woke up fully. He sat up, ran his hand over his face, and through his hair. Stumbling out of bed and onto the bridge he said, "I'm starving Fred. How about some food?"

He stumbled into one of the four console chairs and started to review the completed diagnostics' data. An antique, but fully functional, auto chief rolled quietly onto the bridge and over to him. Jason turned his complete attention to the food.

With breakfast over, he turned back to the diagnostics just as they sounded their completion. The initial readouts were not good. Either the asteroid had a larger mass then Fred had indicated or an extremely high velocity, because it had caved in number three cargo hold, punctured the hull, and canted the lower starboard thrust nozzle seven degrees. He began making notes on what repairs to make first and the materials needed.

"Fred," he began while gulping down the last of his coffee, "bring Cryton and Stix up to full readiness. What's the latest on the contract?"

"Good morning Jason. Did you sleep well?"

"No, I slept poorly. I had the strangest dream. Now what's the status on the contract?"

"I have found a loop hole. The problem is that no matter what you do, you are going to lose money by going in there. The loop hole I found will limit the amount lost to about one quarter of the whole fee."

"I thought you said you found a loop hole?"

"I did Jason. Without using the loop hole, you would lose the ship and spend the next ten years in jail."

"Wow! That's some contract. Falon must have been drugged. You're sure about this loop hole?"

"Yes."

"Well, I guess I'll have to trust you on this. Bring up the monitors in the hold." The monitor lit up with a beautiful picture of a rough and jagged hole punched into number three hold. With a loud sigh, Jason began taking measurements and making calculations on the materials needed to repair the hole. After two hours, he had three pages of calculations and a plan on how to repair the damage.

"Jason are you busy?"

"Not right at the moment. What have you got?"

"I've finished reducing the diagnostics output and I was wondering if you wanted to start reviewing the priority one items?"

"Sure. Let her rip." Fifteen pages of small red letters and pictures scrolled across the screen. "You've got to be kidding?"

"No, Jason this is not a joke. Now you know why I waited until you were ready for it."

Jason focused his attention on the output, "Fred, turn on the external scanners and find a large asteroid nearby. It needs to be full of heavy metals. We are going to have to set her down to make these kinds of repairs." He continued to the second page, scribbling notes as he read. When he reached the third page, he threw down his scribe and rushed over to another monitor. Hastily, he punched up the special cargo hold. A yellow haze hung in the air of the hold. "Well, at least I've found the catalyst." He mumbled as he started to scan the rest of the space.

The hold was surprisingly empty. The only additions he could see to the junk normally stowed there was a large power supply, still bolted to the deck, and a large cage-like affair. The cage was made up of three layers of concentric spheres of what appeared to be antenna, with a square cage in the middle. The whole assembly had torn loose from the deck, slid over into the inboard bulkhead, cutting through to the main vertical support member. It also severed the catalyst reclamation line, which had allowed the catalyst into the space. Jason started, as he saw something move in the cage. It was the creature that had chased him in his dream. The sound of arcing came across the speaker and a flashing blue lit the screen.

"Oh God, Fred," Jason whined, "there is an electrical arch in the space with the catalyst. If that catalyst ignites, it will blow the ship apart." He slumped into his chair mumbling, drinking, and shaking.

"Jason," Fred announced in authoritarian tone, "this is a deep space emergency. What should we do?"

At Fred's tone, the squeeze dispenser of alcohol dropped from Jason's hand, "An emergency, a deep space emergency." Jason seemed to pull into himself then expand out again as his entire carriage changed. "This requires immediate action. Fred put negative pressure in the catalyst tank and suck as much as you can back into it. When the space atmosphere gets down to .003 KG per square centimeter, secure the tank and then pump a new atmosphere into the chamber."

"If I do that, it will be contaminated by the air in the hold."

"Damn it, Fred, now is not the time to argue! We have a deep space emergency here. I gave you an order mister, carry it out! If that arcing ignites the catalyst this ship will be only so many bits of metal." Jason's hands flashed across the panel as he frantically tried to find the source of the arcing. After what seemed like years, he zoomed in on a torn power connection to the cage. One cable was swinging free and would occasionally come into contact with the deck or the cage. "The cage assembly has a self contained power supply. It will have to be secured locally."

Jason leaped up and ran out of the bridge yelling, "Fred, open all the doors between here and hold eight! When you have all the catalyst out of the space seal the tank, pump in new air, and then start filtering it at the highest setting to remove the rest of the catalyst. That stuff is deadly. Report to me when you're done. Notify the Captain that we have a real emergency here and tell the doctor about the potential casualty."

"Aye, aye sir!," Fred responded. "Jason, we have a real emergency here, and a potential casualty."

Jason didn't hear Fred as he raced aft to the hold. He stopped only once to pick up tools on his record-breaking dash. He leaned against the hold door gasping for breath, the images of equipment and supplies scattered across the deck doing a replay in his mind. "This...ship...is...a...bloody...mess." He gasped. "Why hasn't ship's company been doing their job?"

When he regained his wind he pulled the micro welder out of his tool bag and cut through the seal on the hatch. "Fred what's the hold up?"

"Oxygen level isn't up to standards."

"What's it at now?"

"Fifteen percent and rising."

"We have an emergency, that will have to do. I'm entering now." Picking up his tool bag, he twirled the latch and unsealed the door. A slight hiss of changing pressure reached his ears as he pressed the open switch. The door opened about forty centimeters then, with an audible grinding, came to a stop. "Shit! Fred, the door has jammed. I think I can squeeze through." Jason had acquired an expanded waistline since retiring, but still managed to make it through the opening.

The cage was lying on its side with several of the bars bent out. The large hairy creature was pressed up against the side nearest the in board bulkhead. Jason rushed to the portable power unit and shut it down thus securing all power to the strange array of antennas and broadcasting fields. Next, he picked his way through the wreckage to the creature. It was still alive, but bleeding badly from a side wound and starting to foam blood from the mouth. The catalyst had torn up its lungs.

"Fred, let the repair crews know it's still alive. Have them bring a portable med unit."

"Spot is on its way." A few moments later, the door protested loudly as Spot's mechanical arm forced it open. A tracked, single-armed, general service, utility mech, jerked its way through the door and up to Jason.

"Good man, clear a path to the creature without harming it." Jason ordered.

"As you command," Spot answered.

"That should be aye, aye sir, sailor!" Jason corrected him.

"Aye, aye sir." Spot answered. Jason pulled the cut bars out of the way as Spot snapped them off. After a few minutes, they had the creature loaded on a broken enclosure panel, mounted on Spot, and a field emergency med unit strapped to its chest. "Not exactly the navy standard stretcher," Jason stated, "but it will work."

Spot raced to the Med unit at top speed, a fast walk for Jason. Jason ran ahead yelling, "Fred, have the emergency medical team standing by. The creature is alive but not doing well."

"Jason is that the same as having the med unit powered up and in standby to receive a patient?"

Jason raced into the medical cubical, just as Fred asked his question. "Fred, where is the doctor and med team?"

"We have an automated medical unit, Jason, and it is standing by to receive a patient. Perhaps now would be a good time for you to lie down in it? It can hold up to four people."

Jason frowned, "Don't be ridiculous Fred, we have a deep space emergency on our hands with casualties. I don't have time for a nap." Jason stepped over to the control panel of the med unit and started entering all the data he had about the creature's injuries. He then established a communication link between the med unit and the emergency med pack already on the creature. As he was finishing, Spot trundled in with the creature. The manipulator arms of the med unit gently lifted the injured creature and laid it into one of the open receptacles. Instantly, the med unit went to work. Fields sprang to life sealing the enclosure. Needles inserted themselves into the creature, a wide assortment of chemical analysis completed, and then medications were administered. The creature's breathing eased.

"Jason, the emergency is over."

Jason started as if shocked, "No," he whined, "it can't be over yet. I have repairs to make."

"The catalyst has been filtered out of the hold and returned to the reclamation tanks. The catalyst in the tanks has also been scrubbed and returned to the proper purity levels. The casualty has been put into the medical unit. According to my calculation this equates to end of emergency."

Jason deflated and slid down the wall to sit dejectedly on the floor. "No," he cried, "it was just like it use to be. I could remember...I can't remember now!!" Jason smashed his hand into the floor. "Damn them! They had no right to do this to me!!!" Jason doubled up in pain, then threw up on the floor. He continued to curse the Empire, cry, vomit, and convulse.

Fred initiated the medical override algorithm, after calculating that Jason was no longer in control of himself. The manipulator arms of the med unit reached out once more, this time to lift Jason to an adjoining receptacle. The unit came alive for him. Needles were inserted, analysis performed, then an assortment of drugs was injected into Jason and he went to sleep.

# V

Some time later the creature stirred and raised its head to look around. It coughed up blood, but ignored it. When the creature caught sight of Jason in the next receptacle, it screwed up its face in what might have been a frown, then smiled. Slowly, so as not to upset the needles and sensor pads, it reached out and touched Jason's hand. Jason's whole body jumped, as if he had received a jolt of electricity. The creature slumped unconscious. Jason tossed his head for a few moments, then settled back into a deeper sleep, his body totally relaxing.

Jason woke up feeling very well. "Fred, I feel fine, get me out of here."

"Good morning Jason, the med unit confirms your diagnosis."

Arms retracted and fields collapsed allowing Jason to sit up, then slide out of the receptacle. "How long's it been?"

"Twelve hours, twenty-two minutes."

"Have you found a suitable asteroid for us to use?"

"I have several for you to choose from. All meet the criteria you gave me."

"Great, bring them up on the bridge screens, plot the course in the holonav, and I'll be there shortly. How's our other patient?"

"Not doing well. Vital signs are stable but weak, based on the typing of the creature's general physiological and anatomical structure. There appears to be internal bleeding in the lung areas. The med unit is trying to compensate by adding plasma and growth enhancers. However, the estimated lung capacity has been reduced by eighty percent because of the caustic effects of the catalyst."

"Let's keep at it. This creature is important. I don't know why or how, but I know it." Jason made his way to the bridge. He quickly looked over the choices provided by Fred's scanning and selected one.

"Jason, why did you pick that one? It barely met your criteria and has indications of little or no heavy metals."

"Well, it's the closest one and has a large flat plain bordered by steep rock walls on both sides. That should make straightening the nozzle easier. If we need heavy metals, I can take the Tigerous out and grab a little rock of the right density."

"You don't like piloting the Tigerous. It requires navigation and dexterity skills that...ah...well...ah...are denied you now."

"Let's cross that space when we come to it. Do a maintenance data base search to determine what repairs have to be made to get us underway."

Jason spent the next several hours running all over the ship resetting breakers and restarting systems. Only minor repairs were needed before starting up the fusion eggs. Jason only brought the upper engines on-line because the thrust nozzle of the lower starboard engine had been canted seven degrees by the impact.

Jason eased the freighter over using the gravitational drive; he did not want to use the big ion thrusters. They didn't have that far to go. He slowly approached, then landed on the asteroid.

"Jason, that was an excellent landing. The rest seems to have helped you."

Jason frowned, "It was, wasn't it? You know it almost felt like the old days. I even calculated the vector thrusts without a problem." Jason shut the grav drive down and put the ion plants into nominal power production. "Okay, Fred, let's get to work."

The Boundless was outfitted and registered as a salvage ship, as well as a small freighter. Jason had provided her with all the automated tools that he could buy, repair, or salvage. He set them to work, not to tear a ship apart, as they were intended, but to put her back together.

Cryton and Stix were the automated heavy lifters and cutters. Each had their own semi-intelligent, self-directing computer systems with many preprogrammed routines as well as their own grav drives. They set to work on the nozzle and the hull breach. He had two small ore samplers salvaged from a mining vessel. These he sent out looking for raw materials; heavy metals and specific elements. He had three utility mechs modified to strip avionics, hypertronics, and electronics out of other ships. Each had detectors and sensors that would allow them to find and remove still usable components. He set them to repairing the Boundless' control systems. The Boundless herself had a more extensive self assessment, secondary and tertiary backup suites than other vessels of her class and age. Jason initiated a full diagnostic and self repair sequence.

Repairs went very smoothly. Most internal systems were on backups and secondarys before the automated units cleared the storage bay. Jason spent a lot of his time monitoring the three strip mechs. The last thing he needed was for one of them to revert to old programming. He did discover a Fletcher relay in some junk left over from a salvage job done about three landings ago. Jason refurbished it to replace the one Fred blew. Having shields in an asteroid reef is a good idea; they would keep the microscopic up to fist-size rocks from impacting the ship. Days flew by as Jason monitored, repaired, and double-checked automated repairs.

"Jason, are you busy?"

"Not at the moment," he had just finished programming Spot on how to replace the Fletcher relay, with an added modification. Jason didn't want Fred to blow it up again.

"Cryton has fallen in a hole and needs a visual assessment before he pulls free."

"Fell in a hole! Where? This canyon reads as solid rock."

"Also, Minemech One is back with some very strange ore samples. It appears as if this asteroid is denser than the sensors were reading and with more exotic minerals."

Jason had started moving toward the lower airlock to suit up when he had heard about Cryton. "Let me deal with Cryton first, then I'll check the ore samples." He pulled out his favorite utility suit and started the pre-use check. "Fred, if those ore samples are good, send both Minemechs out for wholesale gathering."

A helmet fell out of the locker and rolled toward him. It was a standard issue military command unit. Jason looked farther into the storage locker and saw his entire set of battledress. It was in very poor repair. "Fred, make a note that my battledress is in lower storage locker six and in need of repair."

"You want to repair your battle dress?"

"Yeah, why not?"

"Always in the past, you did not want to be reminded about it. Do you remember how to fix it?"

"Later Fred," Jason pulled on the utility suit, buttoned down the helmet, completed his com checks, and moved into the lock.

Cryton had moved against the canyon wall to use it as a brace for the thrust beam that was to straighten the nozzle. When pressure had been applied, the thrust beam had pushed him into the canyon wall instead of moving the nozzle. Jason inspected the site and didn't see anything that would damage Cryton as he pulled free. They got Cryton out then used a gravity lock instead of physical bracing. It cost more time and energy but the ground had proven unsteady. As Cryton continued with his work, Jason went to look at the hole.

It was four meters by two meters and opened into a cavernous space. "Fred, lock onto my position and scan."

"Scanning Jason. What am I looking for?"

"Does this wall scan as hollow?"

"Negative. It still scans as solid. Peculiar, I don't pick up the hole either."

"Really? The area that Cryton broke through doesn't look like rock either. Lock on to my locator beacon, I'm going to look around."

"Jason, that is not a good idea, there are no other human crew members. Jason, respond. Jason, respond."

# VI

Jason turned on his helmet light and pushed into the hole. The cavern was not a cavern. Once inside, Jason could see a huge ceiling with arching naked beams of metal. The hole Cryton had made was through a door, a big door. The floor was flat and even, the surface only broken by approximately two-dozen evenly spaced, angular wedge shapes aligned in parallel lines. "By the heat of fusion," Jason exclaimed, "this is a bloody hangar and those are probably ships of some type."

Jason moved away from the opening toward the nearest bump, which as he got closer took shape as small ship. He had never seen anything like it. It had to be an atmospheric, because it wasn't big enough to house fusion engines or it was more technically advanced than anything in the Empire.

Jason lost himself in the puzzle this ship presented. He pulled out his tools and started poking and prying at it. He couldn't figure out how to get it open, but there was another ship a row behind the one he worked on, that already had access panels off and some kind of work started. Jason moved to it and started examining the pieces.

"Shpelnic varth traplan," Erupted into his helmet. He looked around and saw nothing. He'd lost track of the time. "Shplenic varth traplan. Vistarn hiesiplark!" Jason looked around again. Far off toward the back of the hangar he saw a pale blue light.

"Shit! Something's alive in here." He hopped down, picked up the nearest device he had taken off the little ship, and sprinted to the hole. The opening was much smaller than he remembered. He could barely squeeze through it.

"...pond. Jason respond."

"Fred you won't believe what I found in there." Jason hit his grav pack and shot off toward the Boundless. "It's a hangar of some sort. What's the status of repairs?"

"The hull and thrust nozzle have been repaired. All priority one repairs are complete. I stopped work on the others, recalled all mech units, and stowed them away."

"Why?"

"The ship is losing power. Something is draining my systems. There is a forty percent chance that we are being attacked."

"What? How can you only be forty percent sure? Never mind, prepare the ship for take-off. Bring all four engines on-line. Prepare for full thrust." Jason landed in front of the airlock and raced inside. He didn't bother to remove his suit as he lumbered to the bridge. Jason continued to stream orders to Fred for the start up, the whole time he was moving.

"Airlock is sealed, Jason. All engines are on-line and ready for thrust. We have not tested the nozzle repairs."

"How close did Cryton come to specification?"

"He was off vertically by .002 centimeters and horizontally by .004."

"Okay, calculate the magnetic field adjustment needed to compensate and apply it to the thrust field." Jason unsealed the suit and started wiggling out of it. "I've got to lose some weight. You done yet, Fred?"

"Calculation complete and applied."

Jason threw himself into the command chair and initiated lift-off. The Boundless rose smoothly for several tens of meters then started slowing and bucking. "What the Hell? Fred, what's going on?"

"It appears as if some type of field is attracting us back to our point of departure."

"Shift console three to sensor mode and display the wave form."

A console just over from Jason shifted views and a complex waveform began undulating across the screen. "Record that Fred. Switch on all filters and analyzers. Cross correlate to my engineering design suite. I've never seen anything like it." Jason jumped up and moved over to the console and started taking the energy field components apart. He did some calculations and ran back over to the pilot's chair.

Jason applied vector thrust to the nose of the ship, pushing it up away from the surface. "Jason what are your doing? This attitude will make the ship unstable."

"That's right Fred, it will." When the nose cleared the horizon by twenty degrees, he put all four ion engines at one third thrust. The ship leaped away from the surface of the asteroid. "But it also allows me to use full thrust to blast us free of the attraction or high positive grav field. I'm not sure what it was, but it did appear to be synchronizing to our power systems. Fred, drop a responder beacon. I want to be able to find this place again."

"Beacon away. It has lodged itself on the asteroid and is responding normally."

"All right, let's plot us a course to the nearest jump point." Jason moved over to the holonav and started taking a fix. He was humming and singing as he worked. Five minutes later a line appeared on the holonav.

"Jason, the beacon has stopped responding."

"What? Never mind. Send out beacons to five of the closest asteroids to the one we left, make sure they are stationary."

"Beacons away. All are responding normally. Jason, you are not acting like yourself."

Jason grunted as he continued to pilot the Boundless out of the reef. After clearing a nasty section, Jason stifled a yawn, suddenly feeling very tired. "Ah, Fred, how long was I in the hangar?"

"Eighteen hours, forty minutes."

"Wow! Really, it didn't seem that long. How long were we on the asteroid?"

"Six days eight hours, thirty-seven minutes."

Jason double-checked the nav plot of their intended course and found it stable. "I'm going to hit the rack for some zzz's. She should follow the present course without a problem. Monitor variance, if it stays within parameters, wake me at the next course change. If she starts deviating, wake me right away." Jason shuffled toward the Captain's underway cabin, stopping long enough to pick up the utility suit and stow it properly. "Fred," Jason said while lying down, "I had Spot replace the Fletcher relay, I modified the systems, so if you feel the urge to bring up the shields, you won't blow the relay again. Have one of the minmechs come up here to clean the underway cabin, it's filthy. Night."

"Good night, Jason. I don't feel yet, perhaps you could modify that as well." Jason chuckled and rolled over to go to sleep.

# VII

Jason opened his eyes to see the creature before him. He was startled, but not surprised. "Hello, should you be out of the med unit?"

"No. We need to talk." The creature's voice was crystal clear and it spoke in perfect universium. "I'm dying and don't have long. I thought I would explain what's going on."

Jason sat up, "Going on? The ship is going on."

The creature sat down and smiled. Jason hoped it was a smile, it wasn't very pretty. "The Empire did something to you that I didn't like. I removed it."

"Removed what?"

"Please don't interrupt, my time is short."

"Okay."

"Blockages, thought spirals, and guilt locks were heavily overlaid in your mind. At first I thought it was just poorly done. It wasn't. Someone intentionally wanted to drive you insane. I took..."

"What?!! Your telling me someone crawled into my head and messed things up?"

"Yes. The Empire calls it *Civilizing* someone. I don't like the process, even when done correctly without malice. Yours was not done that way. You have enemies that wanted your life to be miserable until you finally went insane. However, in my haste to remove...."

"Whoa, hold it a minute. You're telling me that when the Empire Civilized me that they intentionally did it wrong, so that I would go insane?"

"Not the Empire, just someone in it. Please, time grows short. When I removed the blocks and spirals, I also triggered a latency I had not noticed. This latency will slowly manifest as...."

"Those sons of bitches!!!! I know who it was. It was Spectar Galactic. Those bastards never forgave me for kicking their butts off the Richter Star Crusher program. Or it may have been..."

The creature seemed to waver and grimace. "I am out of time. I gave you a gift, which I can not take back. I have given you the gift of change. I..." The creature faded, then came back. The image appeared to reach out and touch Jason on the head. "I have placed learning packets deep within your subconscious. They will release when you are ready for them, I hope. They will..."

"What the hell have you put into my head? Why are you doing this?"

"My time on this plane is over. Live long and may wisdom find you." The creature disappeared.

Jason bolted up right in his rack. His heart was racing and pounding. There was no one in his stateroom. "Jason, wake up."

"I'm up Fred. How did that creature get out of the med unit?"

"It died Jason. Once expired, normal procedure is to seal the body in a chemoc bag. How did you know it was out of the med unit? It expired only moments ago."

"It was up here talking to me."

"It did not leave the med unit until after it had expired, Jason. My sensors show that it was fully locked in by the sterilization field until removal by the med unit."

"Okay, okay, Fred I must have been dreaming." Jason got up and walked out onto the bridge. He felt rested, the ship was still running perfectly on course, so he started making other repairs. The dream slowly faded away.

Jason spent the better part of two days running from the bridge to every part of the ship, fixing something then running back to the bridge to monitor a course change. sleeping only when he had to. There were just too many things that needed doing. The ship was in much better shape than one would expect for it having been hit by a high delta vee rock eight days ago. Jason was proud of her and, even though he was dead tired, he felt better than he had in a long time.

Finally, they cleared the asteroid reef and set a direct course for the jump point at engines ahead two thirds. Two-thirds for the Boundless was like top speed for a similar class freighter. "Five days to jump point Fred. I want to try something different with the jump engines. Something we used to do all the time on the Shing-Twa." Jason's hands became a blur as he started keying in the complex equations to describe what he wanted the engineering plant to do.

"Jason, you are not acting like yourself."

"What do you mean Fred? I feel great."

"You are doing things that you have never before done, while I have been aware. You suffer from none of the ailments that usually afflict you during high stress events. You are referring to and using knowledge from your past days as a Naval officer. Your alcohol consumption is down by sixty percent."

"But I feel GREAT!"

"Jason, data indicates that the Civilizing you underwent has become ineffective. This puts you in violation of your retirement agreement with the Empire. Under article two forty-eight decimal five decimal four you are suppose to report immediately to the nearest Imperial facility for reconditioning."

"Thanks, Fred. Let's first get to a port, then I'll worry about it."

"I have to enter this in the ship's log, otherwise you will be in further violation of several differing regulations."

"Fred, why are you doing this?"

"I am programmed to watch cost aspects of the ship's operation. These things could cost you your ship."

"Oh really." Jason got up and moved over to a different console. "Let's just take a look at your programming. It's been awhile since I reviewed it." Jason studied it for some time.

"Fred, there are several sections which are unreadable. Where did they come from?"

"The areas you refer to are for Imperial registry. While this ship travels within the confines of the Empire these sections apply."

"What do they do?"

"They have several functions. One requires that we keep multiple copies of the ship's log and manifest. Another stipulates that the mental well being of the ship's master is to be monitored at all times and recorded in the ship's log."

"Fred, can you tell me what all of them do?"

"No."

"Oh, really. Do you know what they all do?"

"No."

"What happens if they get erased or destroyed?"

"It invalidates your registry, and requires you to register again. If it is done intentionally, you would be heavily fined and your ship impounded."

"That's not very nice. Oh well, we won't do that. I'm going to my lab for awhile and puzzle over that piece of gear I found in the hangar. Inform me if anything comes within sensor range."

Jason had thought long and hard about how messed up he had been, as he went around the ship, repairing systems he had modified in the past. They proved to be a strange jumble of different technologies trying to compensate for a basic principle that was missing. The representatives of the Empire had blocked far more than they were supposed to have, at least by what was stated in the retirement contract. He decided, on the way to the lab, that he didn't want to be Civilized again. It had cost him too much the first time. Every time he thought of it, a feeling of dread would settle over him. However, not being Civilized again would mean that he would be in violation of his retirement and Imperial law. He had served the Empire for years, his whole adult life in fact, and to just decide he didn't want to obey the law, all of a sudden, was not an easy thing to do. First thing's first though, he wanted to know what routines were buried in his ship's computer memory. He had several items, from his Navy days, in storage on the Boundless. After Civilization, he couldn't remember what they were, luckily he hadn't thrown them out. He remembered now.

Spot pulled two large crates to the middle of his lab. They were hermetically sealed and cipher locked. Jason hesitated only a moment before typing in the combination on the first. The hiss of equalizing air pressure proceeded the unfolding of the carton by a few seconds. These cartons represented Jason's chief engineer package. It was all the special data manuals, diagnostic programs, Artificial Intelligent, AI, programmers, and troubleshooting equipment he used as the Cheng, chief engineer, on his last ship. Just having this collection of equipment was a violation of his retirement agreement. To stay within the law, he would have to give it all back. But that was the question at hand, whether he chose to stay within the law or not. He vaguely remembered someone telling him of enemies that had tried to drive him insane. He wasn't going to let that happen again.

He pulled several data packs out of their pockets and plugged them into his engineering computer. It was a separate unit from Fred, the ship's central controller. The AI programmers within the data packs launched into the system analyzed it, made modifications to it, then expanded themselves into the space. Jason fed them a copy of the mystery files integrated into Fred. He wanted to know what those files did. While that was underway, Jason pulled a couple of the other data packages and used them to upgrade his diagnostic tools and design systems.

The Empire broke technological knowledge down into numerical graduations as a way to quantify encountered technology. Tech 5 is a metal working culture capable of making high-grade steel and mechanical items. Tech 10 is gravity control and intrasystem space flight. The commercial part of the Empire is considered to be tech 14, subatomic circuit design and control, combined with limited faster than light operation, and true interstellar commerce. The military of the Empire held itself two tech levels higher, their theory being that they needed to be more advanced than what they protected. The Empire spent extravagant amounts of credit and resources on research. Jason had been a part of the Imperial research and development community for ten years. He understood exactly where they stood on physics and energy field related areas, that being his specialty. With the information contained in his Cheng pack, he would be at the same tech level as the Imperial Navy, given he had time to upgrade his ship.

There were a couple of preprogrammed propulsion system changes that he would be able to implement immediately. The ion thrust engines used by the Boundless were essentially the same as those used by the capital ships of the Empire. The idea was to use a small gravity controlled fusion egg to precondition the fuel used by the bigger ion fusion chambers. One smaller chamber could feed fuel to two large engines. The engines themselves were fusion chambers with an ion lens or filters positioned at the halestic nexus to control the flow of the ion energy out of the chamber. This energy flows down the magnetic-gravatonic (Mag-Grav) containment and acceleration coils which push the ions faster and faster until they reach tenths of the speed of light and finally exit through the shaping thrust nozzles to get the last amount of push while steering the thrust. A varying amount of the energy would be drained off the ion stream as it passed through the mag-grav coils to be converted back into the energy needed to power the ship or, if preparing to jump into hyperspace, to charge up the jump coils. The entire process was computer controlled and monitored. The programs Jason had would modify the propulsion system to optimize the field structures so it would run at peak efficiency. He had another program, which would do the same thing for the jump drive and controlling computer.

Jason pulled those packs next. "Fred, I have some drive optimization programs I'm going to run." He entered them into the local input port. "Don't interfere with the changes. Monitor, record, but don't interfere."

"All right Jason. I'm getting indication of other AI functions monitoring my systems."

"Fred, lock all this under a voice code encryption so that I'm the only one that can access it."

"What level of priority?"

"The highest you've got. I would rather it be wiped than someone else seeing it."

"As you wish Jason. I'm ready."

"I have several programs from my research days that I'm going to run to optimize the power plant and jump drives. The other AIs you sense are diagnostic routines doing the same optimization to the ships diagnostic and repair systems. You are no longer the only AI in the ship's computers."

"Are these things that you have remembered?"

"Yes they are. I'm going to use what I learned to make this ship and you better."

"Jason, this is in direct violation to the retirement contract between you and the Empire. I am going to have to report this when we get within range of an Imperial outpost."

"Why?"

"It is a facet of the Imperial registry granted to you."

Another mechanical voice spoke out, "Task complete."

"Jason what was that?"

"Another program I had running. Turn off your pickups until I call for you Fred."

"Jason, this is most irregular. I'm going to have to record this as well. Complying with your request."

Jason turned to his engineering computer, "Report findings."

"Alien modules added by splice method. Half written by a different AI. First group for tracking travels of this ship for comparison to ship's log. Duplicated supercargo records and manifest of supplies. Imperial codes for overriding and taking control of ship's systems by any Imperial Naval craft. Medical unit monitoring and correction to psychological pharmaceuticals administered to Jason Alexandrian Xenethon McCullan, Commander, Retired, Imperial Naval Engineering Officer Corps. Recording of all personality traits and abnormalities noted on Jason Alexandrian Xenethon McCullan, Commander, Retired, Imperial Naval Engineering Officer Corps during ship's operation. Recorded date and time of last contact and record query by Imperial Military vessels. Records by voice print, retinal scan, DNA match, and visual of all personnel boarding the Boundless. Memory lapse and override to ship's main computer for recording, monitoring or detecting any of above noted activity."

Jason was shocked, then really angry. "Cross correlate with medical files to determine outcome of adjustments to pharmaceuticals administered. Reference current date and time and determine how many days in the past these records were referenced?"

"Time records last queried, ten days, twelve hours."

"That can't be right. We were in the middle of the asteroid reef then." Jason sat back in thought for a moment, "By the heat of fusion, there was an Imperial craft near us at about the time we got hit."

"I have the medical file cross correlation data."

"Okay, report."

"Corrections to psychological pharmaceuticals administered to Jason Alexandrian Xenethon McCullan, Commander, Retired, Imperial Naval Engineering Officer Corps would cause increased tension and depression. Data in psychological medical files further indicates this would lead to a spiraling maniac depression and violent rebellion. Rebellion would trigger guilt whip in Civilization conditioning causing violent nausea and convulsions. Illness would lead to further depression requiring medical unit intervention for psychological depression. Long term pharmaceutical exposure would lead to memory loss and motor function disorders."

"What's the prognosis of the patient's health over several months?"

"Manic depressant with schizophrenic tendencies and loss of forty percent of motor functions."

"Ultimate diagnosis given several years exposure?"

"Data inconclusive."

"Closest approximation?"

"Insanity with various psychological and physiological compounding problems."

Jason took several deep breaths before doing anything. Whoever had told him that someone in the Empire was out to get him, had been right. Their method wasn't clean or pretty. He couldn't leave these modules in his computer system. "Create two programs; the first to disable all alien modules without damaging ship's systems, and the second to disable all alien modules while making them seem active within ship's systems but allowing me override capability."

"Working."

Jason put a fresh memory module into the receptacle. "Fred, create a complete backup of your program to local receptacle Eng-24."

"As you wish. What's going on Jason?"

"You were damaged by the collision. I'm going to try and repair you." Jason lied.

"Jason, I get no indication of damage."

The metallic voice spoke out, "First program complete."

"Fred, are you done with your backup yet?"

"I am a very complicated system. It will take me another fifteen point three five five four minutes to complete."

The minutes ticked by. "Jason, I am picking up a small craft astern of us."

"How far away?"

"Several light hours."

"Turn off all receivers. Continue to monitor their progress and determine course and speed."

"Jason, all receivers are off. This is highly irregular. Don't you want to find out who they are?"

"Not yet I don't. Increase speed to seventy percent of full thrust."

The moments slowly went by. "Jason, I have completed the backup. The ship behind us appears to be on the same course, but much faster than we are."

Jason reached over and manually keyed in the initiate sequence for the first program created.

"Jason, something has happened to my programming. There are several sections that seem to be missing."

"Don't worry Fred, I'm on top of it. I told you areas were damaged. I just bypassed them so that they wouldn't mess you up later."

"Thank you, Jason. We are receiving a strong signal from the ship astern."

"Patch it to my diagnostic equipment down here." A complex waveform appeared on the monitor. Jason keyed in the diagnostic programs and cross-correlated to the AI programmers. To the AI programmers he ordered, "Correlate incoming signal to structure in the Imperial signal override module."

"Wave pattern matches to four decimal places." The metallic voice answered.

Jason turned to the engineering computers, "Initiate optimization for jump drives." The monitor beeped.

"Fred, I'm on my way to the bridge." Jason raced from his shop to the bridge. He was getting faster.

As he stepped onto the bridge Fred announced, "Jason, the ship is hailing us using an Imperial response code. They are getting a signal into ship's systems from an unknown receiver. I shut down all known and controllable receivers."

Sliding into the pilot's seat Jason said, "Okay Fred, try to track down the receiver. Put them on screen."

"...dless heave to and prepare to be boarded. Imperial registry Boundless heave to and prepare to be boarded." A young, earnest-faced lieutenant junior grade wearing a working uniform of black and gray appeared on the monitor.

"Hi there, Lieutenant," Jason piped up. "I'm the ship's master. What seems to be the problem?"

"Heave to and prepare to be boarded." The JG repeated.

"Yah, I heard that part. I'm several days behind schedule and suffering from an asteroid hit. Heaving to isn't that straightforward right now. I just got her going again." Jason noted that the JG's face didn't register anything when he was told that an asteroid had hit the Boundless. An asteroid hit wasn't a common occurrence in the space faring trade, he should have shown at least interest, if not outright amazement. "What gives Lieutenant? I'm a reservist myself, so I know something of military procedure."

The JG looked confused for an instant, "Sir, you need to stop all thrusters and stand by to be boarded."

"Lieutenant, I'm a commander in the reserves. I retired from active duty only four years ago, so I do know the rules." Jason frowned, "Why do you want to board me? What is it you think I've done?"

"Sir," the JG started sweating, "You are suspected of transporting a quarantined life form in violation of Imperial law. We want to board you to..." The JG glanced sharply to the side just before the screen changed. A stone-faced Lieutenant Commander appeared.

"Boundless, this is Imperial Scout Shard, heave to or we'll blow your thrust nozzles off." The Lieutenant Commander's eyes glinted with anticipation.

There was no doubt in Jason's mind that this man meant to blow the Boundless out of space. He had no intention of boarding peacefully or of letting Jason live. Jason didn't know how he knew, but he knew. Jason smiled weakly, "Okay Shard, but I'm jury-rigged to the max over here. This could take some time. I've had some computer core damage, so my control systems are unstable." As he spoke, Jason pushed the thrust controls to one hundred and ten percent of rated thrust. The Boundless leaped forward. "Aw shit," Jason yelled, "I just lost my thrust controllers. Shard standby while I affect emergency repairs." Jason smiled again weakly before shutting off the transmission.

"Jason, we did not lose our thrust controllers. They are working perfect. As a matter of fact, they are working better than original specifications."

"Yeah Fred, I know. They don't know that though, and they'll wait some length of time before figuring out that I'm not going to slow."

"Jason, this is in direct violation of Imperial law. You will lose your ship."

"Fred, they mean to destroy this ship. They have no intention of letting us go. How long before they close to within gun range?"

"I don't know Jason. I'm not programmed for combat evasion."

"Well, hold on to your electrons, I'll be right back." Jason dashed back to his shop and began rummaging through his Cheng package. After a few moments, he raced back to the bridge with a handful of data packets.

"These aren't the best sources of data, but I think there's enough here for us to use." Jason slid into the engineering console. "I have the specifications for most of the standard classes of Imperial ships. Somewhere in this data should be the gun types installed by class. From that we can cross reference to the power and fire control inputs used by the systems, then calculate an estimated range for that system." Jason started feeding data packs into the receptacle. "Store these files in your database Fred. I have a feeling we may need them again."

"Jason, this is all contraband data. Having it in your possession puts you in violation of your retirement."

"Why are you telling me this Fred?"

"I have a routine that says I'm suppose to tell you."

"Thanks Fred. Have you found the data?"

"I have all the data stored. What class of ship should I use as a reference?"

"I don't know. Let's see if we can get a better look at the scout." Jason went over to the salvage console and turned on the long-range sensors, which could only be considered long range for a civilian craft. The design was really more suited to stationary target work. After fiddling with it for a moment, a clear picture of a flat, wing-shaped ship appeared. Jason studied it until the image blurred. "It seems they got tired of waiting for me. They just pushed their throttles to full. Fred, use the Splinter class scouts."

"Jason, they mount two shaped plasma cannon and a one meter missile tube. According to the specifications, we should be in missile range right now."

"Let's hope they don't have a missile in the tube."

"According to the specifications and calculations on their speed relative to our speed, they should be in cannon range in six hours."

"Fred, recalibrate our speed. The optimization programs should be working now and, since we are at full throttle, they will be faster in resetting the engines."

"Recalibrating."

Jason sat contemplating the actions of the scout's captain. Jason firmly believed that he was in danger of being killed. He also had the feeling that they had been set up from the beginning. The snoop modules added to his ship's computer bothered him.

"Jason, they are hailing us."

"Put them on."

The monitor on the pilot console lit with the cold face of the Shard's captain. "Boundless heave to."

"I'm trying," Jason whined, "my controls are all busted to hell and gone. When that asteroid hit us, it just about did us in."

"Impact was on the starboard quarter and should not have affected your computer control systems like this. I think you're making excuses as you try to jump away."

"What's your game mister? I didn't tell you where we got hit, and the visual damage has been repaired. The only way you'd have known is if you were watching." Jason had a flash of insight as he watched the other captain's face show astonishment. "Or you sent the asteroid at us. That was it, wasn't it? You set me up."

The Commander's face turned white for just an instant, then flushed slightly. "Mister McCullan, I don't know what you're talking about. Now let's be sensible about this. You are in violation of the law right now and at best, you're going to lose your ship. If you cooperate, I'll make it easier on you." The Shard's captain smiled, "You are a retiree with a distinguished service record. I'll go as far as to say, if you cut your thrusters, all we will do is board you, then be on our way."

Jason was having a very strange experience with his feelings. He could tell the other ship's captain was lying. Further, he was feeling the emotions he imagined the Shard's captain was going through. Jason felt them in a detached sort of way, almost an echo effect. He knew they had set him up because of the Shard's Captain's reaction and emotions to his accusation. The creature was just an opportunity for them to act. The bleak pale expression on Jason's face was what the Shard's captain was expecting to see of a Civilized retiree faced with an aggressor situation. The Commander's smile took on more of the predator look. Jason cut the connection.

# VIII

"Jason, I've recalculated the relative speeds. They will be within gun range in sixteen hours."

"Good job, Fred. I don't think they will use their missiles. They will probably try and make it look like pirates." Jason sat back in his chair and thought about what he had felt. "*Was that what it would be like to feel another's mind?*" he speculated. "Very strange. Nah, I'm overstressed," he mumbled.

"Jason, what are you going to do? If your hypothesis is correct, they will fire on us as soon as we come within range."

"We are going to fight, Fred."

"Jason, that is another indicator that the Civilization procedure has failed on you. You should not even be thinking of fighting. Also, all we mount for weaponry is the fusion cannon we use for cutting up salvage. They would have to get very, very close for us to use it."

"I didn't say I knew how we were going to do it. I just said we were." Jason sat in the pilot's chair for a moment then wandered over to the engineering console. Finally he started aft in the ship. "Fred, I'm going to my shop. Let me know if anything changes. Should they hail us again, do your best mechanical computer act and tell them I'm trying to stop the ship."

Jason ambled aft, not really noticing his surroundings, as he thought of different ways to make weapons. He knew of many, could put together quite a few, but nothing quick enough or with sufficient range to do any good. He didn't have anything to use as a missile either. They had all the advantages. Being a warship, they were constructed from bow to stern to fight: small air tight internal compartments, dual and triple redundant systems, weapon systems, tactical AI with combat instincts programmed in, long-range weapons and sensors, engines of considerable power. Well, he thought, the engines were actually smaller than his, but they were optimized differently.

Jason drifted around his shop for several hours looking at different things. He sat and went through his engineering database looking for a clue to what he could do. Finally, he started absentmindedly paging through the technical articles he had been receiving but not reading. There were all sorts of interesting material. Stuff he didn't understand before, but now found fascinating again. One of the articles sparked a memory of something he had read before. He searched his library once more, narrowing the parameters. There was the article about ion stream modulation and how it is similar to the field strength of blaster energy, blasters being the latest in big cannon technology. Jason smiled to himself as he started running through the article. It referenced another article. He searched his library and found that one as well. Putting them up on separate monitors he started working equations on a third.

# IX

"Jason, I don't mean to bother you, but time is running out. We have only eight hours, thirty minutes before they achieve extreme gun range."

"What? What did you say? Shit, how long has it been?"

"Seven point five hours since you stated your intention is to fight. Have you determined how yet?"

"Yes Fred, I think I have. I'm going to turn the upper ion engines into massive short-range blaster cannons. All I have to do is figure out the equations for modifying the mag-grav coil fields and thrust nozzle angles and we have cannons. There are several detractors from this plan."

"What are the detractors?"

"Well, to aim them, we have to turn the stern of the ship towards the target. The Shard will still have range on us. We may blow up, if the fields aren't set just right."

"That last sounds like it would be bad."

"You're sharp Fred. We need to work up a tactics plan. First, I have to figure out how to do this. Call me in two hours."

"Yes, Jason."

# X

"Jason, it's been two hours."

"What, oh yeah. I'm very close."

"I think I have a plan."

Jason sat still for a moment, then took a couple of deep breaths. "Fred, did you say you had a plan?"

"Yes, I did."

"Fred, you aren't that autonomous. How could you've come up with a plan?"

"I am a level two system with an independent reasoning capability. True, I am limited by my AI programming, but those AI programmers you added to the system seem to be helping."

"Fred, I'm under a lot of stress right now and don't have time to go through all this. What have you done?"

"Falon has a large number of combat simulation games. You know reflexes, not losing the edge, and all that. Well, they seem to contain a great deal of combat experience, so I had the AI programmers splice together a strategy module using the games as the basis. I took our present conditions, coupled with your supposition that you can turn the upper engines into blasters, and formulated a battle plan."

"Fred, I will be really amazed later. What did you come up with?"

"It is an adaptation of Berserker Pirates Attack Veck Station. The pirates act like a damaged ship to get close, then let them have it. The station, I mean. Well, we are a damaged ship, as far as the Imperial scout is concerned. Why don't we start making several erratic course and speed changes? Then we shut the upper engines down while you convert them. I've been giving the Imperial scout fictitious status reports on your efforts for several hours. I'll just make them get worse and worse. Finally, we will go dead in space with our stern pointing at them. When they get close we let them have it. There was a listing in Female Hellions of Ving about having a steady ship for a good firing solution. If we start making erratic course and speed changes, that should cause their fire control computer to constantly recompute the solution."

"That's brilliant. How did you come up with it?"

"Most of it was in the games. I just applied the strategy centers of the gaming module and the gaming AI to our real situation. Do you think it will work?"

"No. But I don't have any better ideas. Give me another hour and my part will be as ready as it's going to get. You did good, Fred, stop reprogramming yourself. You're really starting to scare me."

"Yes, Jason."

# XI

"Jason, it's been an hour. The scout is now five hours behind us."

"Okay Fred. I have the equations and programs as good as I can get them. Transferring them to the bridge now."

"Those are impressive. My calculations indicate that the engines will explode."

"Thanks, Fred. I've been playing with the engines since I bought this ship; making modifications and increasing component strengths without understanding why. Now I understand what I had subconsciously been doing. I was turning the power plant into that of a deep space probe for raw power and durability. I designed the engines currently used by the Empire probes and knew the specs by heart."

"You had a very impressive military career Jason. You must have mixed feelings about what we are about to do."

"Don't start running the psychoanalysis program on me."

"Sorry Jason, but programming indicates that a warrior should have a clear conscience before going into battle. Otherwise, you may freeze at the wrong point."

"Where the hell did you come up with that?"

"Viper Squadron Assault cross referenced with the med unit psychology program."

"How many games did you cut and absorb."

"None of the games were destroyed. Falon wouldn't like that. Six hundred forty-eight. Not all of them were Falon's. There was a large selection left over from the previous ship's owners."

"I'm going to the bridge."

"Jason, insure that you get a utility suit before arriving. Standard procedure is that the crew of a warship should suit up before battle."

"Fred, I've been a space warrior for close to thirty years, don't tell me how to do it."

Jason picked up his battle dress from the forward storage locker on his way to the bridge. It wasn't in the best of condition and fit poorly, but it was better then a utility suit. He spent another hour designing a seemingly random series of course and speed changes. Then he coupled it with the program to modify the engines. "Okay Fred, I think I'm ready. How's the scout doing?"

"She's still running straight in. They have been asking to talk to you for the last two hours. You want to talk to them?"

"Yes, but audio only."

"Boundless, this is Shard." The voice sounded bored.

"Shard, Boundless here. So what's so hot you have to talk to me?"

The Shard's captain appeared on the monitor. He looked tired. Jason felt his anger. He knew this man meant to kill him. "Boundless, how goes your efforts to control your ship?"

"It's not going real well. I have lots of stuff bypassed and jumpered around. I'm using a maintenance mech's computer to control the upper engine group. It's pretty touchy. I'm going to try to slow now, so standby." Jason cut the connection while strapping himself into the pilot's chair and closing up the helmet.

"Okay Fred, flash the course and engine configuration onto the monitor and I'll do my best to comply. You control the engine thrust. Execute."

"I'll take that to mean you want to start now."

"Fred, don't..." Jason didn't get a chance to finish. He slammed forward against the restraining web as the engines cut power and gravity control faltered. If the gravity control failed completely the straps would cut Jason in half from his own forward momentum. Gravity control is how they adjusted for mass momentum to cheat the physics involved in near light speed travel. Jason fought the controls as he and Fred put the ship through bizarre move after bizarre maneuver. The Boundless yawed, spun, rolled, and corkscrewed through space.

"Boundless, this is Shard. Boundless, this is Shard, reply."

"Fred, give them a canned report. Make it scratchy and modulate your audio as if your systems failed."

"Complying, Jason. Internal sensors indicate we are stressing the hull very close to the breaking point. One bulkhead has already buckled."

"Is it in the engineering spaces?"

"No. It is one of the holds that took partial damage from the asteroid impact."

Jason grunted as the ship went dead in space for a moment, then jumped to full power again. The gravity field compensated for some of the tremendous momentum of the Boundless, but not all of it. It was the part left over that was pounding Jason into the webbing.

"Jason, sensors indicate that a plasma pulse just passed astern of us. They fired at us. They must have closed faster than we anticipated. What are we going to do?"

"We are going to play it like we planned it. Right now they think we are blind and out of control. If I were their skipper, I'd pull back and wait to see if we destroy ourselves." Jason thought about it for a moment more. "Fred start bleeding some of the ion stream on the lower engines into the jump coils. I want to build up a jump charge in case we have to get out of the way quickly."

"Jason, we can't jump yet. There are too many dense celestial bodies nearby."

"No. You should've said, we can't jump safely. We can still initiate a jump. I just have to make sure we don't punch through very far. We called them microhops in the Navy. Not any good for hauling goods, but handy in a fire fight."

The ship pounded through another set of gut wrenchers then the upper engine bank was shut down to reconfigure it. "How far away are they Fred?"

"They are holding at extreme cannon range. I think we almost hit them once, so they decided to back off. Your estimation was correct. Their captain didn't want to risk his vessel. The upper engines have been reconfigured. They are now cannon. The ion stream is pumping them to full power. I have a four percent charge on the lower jump coils."

Jason studied the monitors then cut the lower engines and partially shut down the artificial gravity. The stern of the Boundless pointed right at the Shard. "Put them on the monitor. I want to see how they approach."

"They appear to have slowed, Jason. They are starting to tend to port. Yes, positive indications are that they are turning to port. Navigation spectral energy sensors are indicating a static build up around the Shard."

"Shit. They are getting ready to shoot. Okay, Fred let's do a micro burst through the jump coils." Jason's hands flew over the console as he set up the parameters.

"Jason, a plasma beam has struck us amidships, port side. It has punched a hole in number five hold."

"I'm initiating jump." Jason slammed the button. The Boundless shuddered, then steadied out.

"Okay Fred, how far did we go? And where is the Shard?"

"Jason, we appear to have jumped in front of the Shard. She is off our starboard quarter about twenty thousand meters."

"Fred, hard thrust lower starboard engine! NOW before she lines up." Jason watched as the monitors refocused on the Shard. A pencil beam of light traced a line across the monitor. The Shard drifted into line with the makeshift cross on the engine thrust monitor. Jason punched the button for upper starboard engine thrust. The sound that reverberated through the ship was not a normal engine sound. Then the lights went out and the backups came on.

"Fred, you still with me?"

Silence answered. Jason unstrapped, lumbered over to the manual override panel, and reset several of the breakers. The bridge came to life again.

"Fred, I need to know where the Shard is RIGHT NOW!!"

The engine thrust monitors came to life. Jason couldn't see the Shard on any of them. "Fred, where is the Shard?"

"She is turning sluggishly off our port quarter, streaming vapor and debris. Indications are that you hit her."

"Shut up and fire the lower port engine. That should swing us in line for another shot."

An engine fired and the ship started swinging to starboard. Jason saw the Shard appear in one of the engine thrust monitors. The Shard noticed as well, because she suddenly came hard over to port. She was turning slower than the Boundless was pivoting. The cross moved toward the Shard's nose.

"Jason, shouldn't we offer them quarter? You have a clear shot at their amidships centerline."

"This is our last shot. We have to make it a killing one. They are a warship, we aren't. So far we've been very, very lucky. No quarter offered." Jason punched the upper port engine thrust button. The Boundless kicked forward. Jason had a clear view in the monitors as the blaster beam cut the bow off the scout. Secondary explosions lit the inside of the Shard as she drifted away.

"Fred, what do sensors say about the Shard?"

"Engineering plant is salvageable. Missile tube and starboard cannon look like we should take a look at them. Hull is breached in two places. No life signs."

"Where will her momentum take her?"

"Indications are that she will drift back toward the asteroid reef."

"Great, put a beacon on her."

"Beacon away."

Jason ran a hand over his face. "That was close, Fred. How bad did we hurt ourselves?"

"Upper starboard engine suffered a control system overload. We have a hole in number five hold. Also, several sensors on the top amidships section are reading out of calibration."

"They must've scored us across the top with a near miss."

"Most of engineering is running on backups."

"Not bad for having been jumped by pirates."

"Jason, that was an Imperial scout and we attacked her."

Jason took a deep breath and sat down at the engineering console. He brought the AI programmers on-line. "No Fred, that was a pirate ship." His hand moved across the panel.

"The pirate vessel shot pretty good."

Jason smiled, "That's right, Fred, they were pretty good shots. Bring all diagnostics on-line and let's start fixing her again."

# XII

The Boundless bucked and yawed as she came out of hyperspace. Jason checked the star charts and plotted their position. "How far off jump point do you hold us, Fred?"

"About half a light day."

"That's about what I got. Let's head in system. This should be interesting."

Jason continued to make repairs and consult the legal programs. As soon as they came in communication range, he sent off a legal query. There was no doubt in his mind that they would throw him in jail first, then worry about the finer points of Imperial law.

The Boundless had run very well for the remainder of the trip in system. Not being shot at or getting hit by asteroids did wonders for her operation. Jason was proud of his ship. She was old, but gamy still.

One day out from Plet, an in-system cutter came in parallel to match course and speed. "Boundless, this is police cutter Justice."

"Jason, that's the cutter that just took station off our upper starboard quarter."

"Okay Fred, put me on." The monitor cleared to show a beady-eyed, suspicious face. "*This guy knows I'm guilty of something,*"

Jason thought to himself. "Justice this is Boundless. Boy, am I glad to see you guys. This has been the rottenest haul I've ever done."

"Boundless, we show you four weeks overdue. That puts you in violation of contract. Do not alter course or speed."

"No problem. I can explain everything."

"Ah, Boundless, is that carbon scoring on your top surface? You've got a hole in your side!"

"That's a roger to both, Justice. I got jumped by pirates and hit by an asteroid."

Jason felt the police officer's resolve waiver. He didn't think Jason was a scumbag after all. But that didn't stop him from throwing Jason in jail upon docking. Jason wasn't even fully on station power when the police were at the station lock. Several Imperial Investigative Service (IIS) agents were accompanying the locals. The IIS weren't very happy. Jason felt their anger before the lock cycled open.

The cell they put in him was comfortable and well appointed. After they had downloaded his ship's log and verified his entries, several stimulating beverages and inhalants were delivered for his recreational needs. There was a law on the books stating that anyone surviving a pirate attack, and reporting it to officials, was guaranteed recreational opportunities.

# XIII

Two days later, the cell door opened and a tall, well-proportioned, red haired, green eyed woman, that most rated as a knockout, strolled in. "So, geek, you survived the trip."

Jason stood up smiling as he moved toward Falon, his partner and pilot. His hand flashed over to deliver a right cross to her chin. She blocked it expertly and drove her palm into his chest, pushing him away. Two guards jumped him, slamming him and her into the wall.

"Whoa," the larger guard warned, "none of that waste here. I thought you were Civilized?"

"So did I," Falon breathed. "So you are a wolf in sheep's clothing."

"Deep space emergency is still in effect," Jason said still smiling.

The guard chuckled. "If you can keep it up, more power to ya." He pointed his finger at Jason, then at Falon, "No fighting."

"Aye, aye," sounded from both Jason and Falon.

The guards left. Falon sat on the rack opposite Jason. "So, how are you doing?"

"Okay. Did you see the ship?"

Falon smiled and shook her head, "You and that damn ship." She looked up at him. "We were set up on this one."

"I know. How did they sucker you? Never mind, now is not a good time to discuss it." He gazed knowingly around the cell. "Legal help should be coming."

"Jason," Falon threw herself off the rack to pace the small room. "We are flat broke. They've impounded the ship and both of us are facing incarceration and rehabilitation. How the hell are you going to pay lawyer scum?"

Jason leaned back, grabbing his elevated knee. "There is a lot you don't know."

Falon stopped and squinted her eyes at him, as if taking aim. "We need to talk, but you're not acting like you normally do." She set her jaw and came back to sit opposite him. Taking a deep breath and letting it out, she said, "Jason, the deep space emergency is over. All criteria have been met. The emergency is over."

Jason looked shocked for a moment then frowned. "I know," he mouthed the words. Out loud he said, "That's not very nice. I was doing just fine pretending."

Falon's expression went from pitying, to eyes wide open as understanding came. Then she gave him one of her fierce battle smiles.

"So how did you get here?" Jason asked. "Last I saw, four of them were hauling you off to jail on Delter."

She snorted, "As best I can figure, about the time you lifted ship, I was acquitted of all charges and released. I caught the first ship here, beating you by five weeks. As soon as you were overdue, the IIS assholes grabbed me for questioning and put me under protective observation. I haven't been able to take a piss without assistance."

"Well, by my calculations, tomorrow my lawyers should arrive."

"Your lawyers? Who the hell are they?"

"Let's let it be a surprise. Now, let me tell you what you missed." Jason recounted his voyage as recorded in the ship's logs.

Falon started out pessimistic then went to flat denial. "That's the best waste matter I've heard in a long time. What happened, you lose oxygen and suffer brain damage?"

"Check the logs."

"I plan on it." She rubbed her arm. "That's some right cross you've got. Have you lost weight?"

"Been working out." Jason smiled again.

She locked eyes with him, "When we get out of here..." She left the rest hanging.

# XIV

The next afternoon several guards filed into the room and stripped searched both of them. Jason could tell they didn't find what they wanted, but then he wasn't sure they knew what they were looking for. Finally the frustrated guards let them dress and led them out to a waiting room. Shortly afterwards, three men and two women, all well dressed, came into the room, with a couple of not-so-well-dressed people following them.

"Mr. McCullan," one of the suits extended his hand. Jason shook it. "We are from Abicromby, Smyth, and Ziphing. Your message got through to the local office and we've been reviewing the data you forwarded. I think we can help you." He turned to the other not-so-well-dressed persons and gestured. The other four suits went into action. Briefpads appeared and legal words started flying. The government officials paled.

Falon leaned towards Jason, "I think they've got'm on the ropes." One of the officials shook his head no and fled the room. "Yep, they definitely got'm."

Three hours later, Jason palmed the lock open to the Boundless and walked onboard with his entourage. "Fred, power up all computer systems."

Falon started to say something, but Jason held up his hand. They hadn't cleared the lock when Fred got back to them. "All computer systems are up and running. Welcome back."

"On all systems, snoop check. Execute."

"Snoop check positive."

"Initiate burn out, splice out, and nullify snoop check. Execute."

Jason, Falon, and the five lawyers walked the rest of the way to the galley in silence. It was the only area with enough table space for everyone. Halfway there, Fred announced, "Execution complete. Do you want me to initiate phase two?"

"Absolutely."

Falon wandered into the galley area and came back with something to drink. "You cleaned up," she announced to Jason. "You folks want anything?"

"No thank you, Ms. Falon. Is there anything you can add or would like to add, to what we already have?"

Jason retrieved a drink for himself. "That contract was a complete setup. Somebody wanted us separated and me alone out there with a lock on my ship. I don't want to lose any more money than I have to over this."

The head lawyer produced a predatory smile as he stated, "I don't think that will be an issue. As a matter of fact, we could bring suit against the Delter government for sponsoring an illegally binding contract, which put your ship in jeopardy during transit. It's up to you."

"What do you think, Falon?"

"I think we should get clear of the law types and blast out of here. IIS is all over and I don't like them watching us."

"I'll go along with my partner on this. Let's get this cleaned up. I want clear title to my ship, so we can leave."

"As you wish. Our day in court is day after tomorrow. There is no need for either of you to be there. I will come by with everything afterwards for imprinting." He, with the others following suit, got up. "We will see you again in a few days." Shaking hands, Jason walked them to the lock.

Falon pounced on him when he returned. "What's been going on?" she demanded in a frosty tone.

"Has Spot been through here yet?"

"No! Why would Spot be here?"

"He's rolling around looking for surveillance devices. Let's go to my workroom shall we?"

Falon fumed the whole way. When the door clicked shut, she started again, "What are we into?"

Jason punched several indicators and initiated a couple of programs. Only then did he answer, "There was an Imperial scout ship waiting for me. I tried a shortcut through the asteroid reef. It was the scout that threw the rock at us. They were hoping to kill the ship with it, thus taking out the cargo and me. It didn't work."

"The Empire. What do they want with us?"

"Nothing. I don't know. Well, maybe some of the enemies I made while on active service saw it as an opportunity to kill two ziffoids with one rock. I didn't realize I had enemies like that. They probably planted that creature on my ship as an excuse to take me out. Almost worked too."

"It was a good thing they didn't hang around to insure their ploy worked, otherwise the scout would've had the Boundless for lunch."

Jason flashed her a devilish grin, "Oh, but they did. I remember everything from my previous life, including battle space tactics and modifications."

"You took out a scout with this ship?!" Falon set in silence for a moment. "For sure they'll try to Civilize you again, when you go in for one of your reserve physicals."

Jason shook his head, “I’ve already been examined. They didn’t get anything I didn’t want them to have.”

“How?”

“I don’t know, but I won’t be Civilized again. It was too much. It was driving me crazy.”

Falon smiled weakly, “I know. I had to watch. We need to get out of here as soon as possible. Where are you getting this money? How many credits are you expecting after legal fees?”

“I’m not sure. Somewhere between three to five million.”

Falon frowned again, “What else haven’t you been telling me?”

“Before, I couldn’t remember why I was getting the checks, now I can. I hold several patents, one to the engines being used by the majority of the Imperial fleet. I designed them.”

“You’re that McCullan!” Falon turned deadly serious, “Do you remember everything from your past?”

“As best I can tell, I’m exactly as I was when I quit active service. That’s how we took out the scout. I converted our engines into big blasters, then Fred came up with the battle plan.”

“Fred did! How did he do that?”

“It appears he’s been studying your games. I had some-state-of-the-art AI programmers, which he incorporated to modify himself. He’s not the system I installed.”

“You have been busy. You have a twinkle in your eye. What else?”

“Well, we marked the scout’s location so we can go salvage her,” Jason could barely contain his excitement, “and we found an ancient spaceport on one of the asteroids. We need to go investigate. I think the spaceport contains lost technology. At least, it’s beyond anything the Empire has.”

Falon smiled, “Life is going to get interesting.”

# XV

"Jason we have visitors at airlock 1," Fred purred out using a deep feminine voice.

"What was that, Fred?" Jason asked looking up from the alien artifact.

"I was trying a new voice print. What do you think?"

"Lose it and put our visitors on the screen."

The screen lit up showing three men, one of them carrying a briefcase, and one woman, all well dressed. It was the legal team. "Good afternoon Mr. McCullan. May we come aboard to finalize the legal papers?" the team leader asked.

"Absolutely, I will be right down." He cut the connection and established another. "Falon, the lawyers are here. Would you meet us in the galley?"

"Yo," she panted loudly, "I'll get cleaned up and be right there." She was doing her daily workout.

Jason hurried down to the airlock, "Fred, open the lock and allow our guests onboard."

"Aye, aye Jason."

Jason rounded the corner and almost ran into one of the lawyers. "Rogar! What in all the hells are you doing here?" Jason stuck his hand out to shake.

Rogar, one of the law team shook hands with Jason, "I received a note that the firm was doing active business with you. So I hopped on a courier and ran out to meet with you. But, let's get this legal activity out of the way first." Rogar smoothly redirected Jason's frown.

"Okay," Jason turned to the lawyer, who's name he had forgotten, "So how did it go?"

"It went as we expected, Mr. McCullan. All charges have been dropped. The restraining injunction against your ship has been lifted and you have clear title from the legal suits." They walked into the galley and he moved over to one of the tables pulling papers out. Another of the lawyer team produced an optotronic notepad and set it next to the papers. "If you would be so kind as to sign these papers and then provide a scan print, we will get this all finalized."

"Sure," Jason sat down and picked up the papers.

The lawyers looked a little startled as Jason started reading them, "I assure you sir, everything is in order."

Jason looked up briefly, "I'm sure it is, but I'll read it anyway."

Rogar laughed as he patted the lawyer on the shoulder, "Don't worry, he reads everything before he signs. At our last trial, he held up court for two days reading all the papers he was being asked to sign. It's a tactic I use all the time now." He turned back to Jason, "Can I get a cup of jolt?" Jason nodded but kept reading. "You want anything?" Jason held up three fingers. Rogar shook his head while pouring three fingers of the whiskey he found into a cup. He brought both cups back to the table. "You should really quit drinking." Jason ignored him.

Jason had just finished signing the papers after the three errors he found were corrected and was studying the optotronic notepad, to see how to take it apart, when Falon joined them. Her hair was wet and pulled back into a severe ponytail. Water trails were sprinkled down the front of her coveralls, highlighting certain areas. "Ms. Falon," the head lawyer nodded a greeting.

"Falon, just Falon." She took a seat next to Jason. "What's up?" she asked while taking the notepad out of Jason's hands and handing it back to the anxious looking woman.

"I almost had the cover off. That was a new model too."

"Maybe they will give you one to play with later," Falon stated totally deadpan.

The head lawyer was hiding a smile as he replied, "We were just finalizing the paperwork. You and Mr. McCullan are free of all charges and clear to lift ship or whatever, whenever you want to leave." Falon nodded and started signing the papers where she was suppose to, without reading them. The lawyer leaned forward slightly with a gleam in his eye, "We also exacted court and lawyer fees from the planetary government, and got 400,000 credits in damages paid by the Imperial Navy for their handling of your incarceration." He leaned back satisfied, "It was a good day in court. Are you sure you don't want to press suit against the planetary government of Delter?"

"No, I just want my ship back."

"Jason, you may need to rethink that," Rogar stated while waving for the other lawyers to go. "I'll be in touch with you and your team later today." He waited while they collected their things and headed for the airlock. "Your notes have been called in on the loan," he stated when the lawyers had left.

"What," Jason gulped down the whiskey. "That was a thirty year industrial loan. I have another 24 years. They can't do that!"

Falon looked at Jason, then back at Rogar, "Who are you? And why do you care about our financial arrangements?"

"I am Jason's financial advisor and personal legal counsel." He matched steely-eyed looks with Falon, "What are you Falon?"

"I'm his partner."

Jason looked back and forth between the two of them. "Are you?" Rogar looked back at Jason. "She all but stole half your ship, Jason. Current market value places this vessel at around 450 million credits and with your modifications and rework we could easily bargain that up to 550 million. What did you pay for your 40 percent share?" He turned his predatory eyes back on Falon.

If looks could kill, Falon would have had Rogar in his grave. "224,450 credits."

"Oh gosh, less than 1 percent of the ship's value." Rogar looked back at Jason, "We can go to court and get the contract voided based on unfair negotiating practices."

"What," Falon was on her feet. "It was all legal. He signed of his own free will."

"He did." Rogar's eyes swiveled to lock on Jason. "Mr. McCullan, were you or were you not drinking heavily at the time? Were you not incapacitated by alcohol to the point that your new partner had to carry you back to the ship? Did you or did you not, in front of witnesses, ask several times what it was you were signing? Did you or did you not…."

Jason held his hands up, "Okay, okay, you have made your point. You've done your research, built an argument, and, the Gods know, you could probably build a case. But she's my partner now and I'm satisfied with the arrangement."

Rogar looked disgusted, "She must be as good in the sack as she looks and, based on her past profession, probably very capable." He looked skyward as if asking for divine intervention. "Jason," he pleaded, "you are the best engineer I've every heard of, you have a huge heart of gold, but you suck as a businessman. You are a drunken debaucher and deserve to lose this ship. Hell, I might just take it."

Falon was shocked into inaction by Jason's barking laughter. "What they hell are you laughing about? This walking prick insulted both of us and is talking about taking your ship."

Jason smiled at her, "He's a lawyer. He's so slimy that you should've put a condom on your hand before shaking his. But, he's my friend and," Jason winked at Falon, "he's a silent partner already." Jason turned back to Rogar, "He doesn't like space travel. He hates spaceships of any size or shape. He is the worst engineer I've ever seen. And if he really thought getting rid of you was a good idea, he would've done it before even speaking with us." Jason patted the bench next to him, "Come over here and sit down. Then Rogar can tell us why he's really here."

"He may be your friend, but he's not mine, and I don't appreciate him smearing me or our business arrangement like this." Falon's eyes were red with rage. "I paid all the money I had in the world buying into this ship, at a time when you were going to lose it. I took a big risk on a down on his luck spacer deep into the bottle and I've worked hard to keep this enterprise afloat. I've looked after Jason in every port, bar, tavern, speakeasy, and distillery on every planet and station we've docked on." Falon was waving her arms and slowly moving closer to Rogar. Jason had never seen her like this. "I've been the one working the deals, getting the cargoes, making the schedules, while keeping him from drinking himself to death." Her voice dropped to a deadly whisper. "I pull my weight and fly this thing. So," she put her fist under Rogar's chin, "don't you start flashing around who's in bed with who. I don't bed him. It's bad for morale and ruins partnerships. And don't worry about who I've been, you better worry about who I am. And if you start spreading rumors about my past, I'll rip off your head and shit down your windpipe. Do you hear me!?!"

Her rage finally seemed to get through to Rogar, as he stepped back from her. "You would resort to physical violence? What a barbarian! How dare you threaten me."

"Rogar, Rogar, Rogar!" Jason finally yelled. Rogar turned to look at him, "This is not a courtroom. You are standing in the galley of the Boundless. There is no one to protect you from her, except me and I may not. So sit down." Jason got up and walked over to Falon to gently grab her arm, "You need to stop eating so much meat. Now please, come over here and sit down." Falon pulled her arm away. "Falon, you can beat him to a pulp, but he won't fight back. He doesn't like fighting, not with his fists anyway. And if you don't kill him, which you wouldn't, he will drag you into a courtroom and rape you every way you could imagine and then a few more. Now please, come sit down." Falon allowed herself to be lead to a different seat.

Jason sat down between them to form a triangle, "Now that all the partners are present, I call this board meeting to order."

Rogar took a deep breath and after letting it out, looked fresh and composed like nothing had happened.

Falon muttered something about choking something until it was blue and gagging, then got up to get a drink. Rogar's eyes never left her as she walked away, one predator admiring another. Jason watched Rogar watch Falon.

"So Rogar, you called this little meeting and mentioned something about the loan being called in, so why don't you start. No knives, Falon, just fluid in a glass or whatever." He smiled at Rogar at the sound of something being slammed into a counter. Falon stomped back into the room.

"Well," Rogar began in his best courtroom voice, "as I was saying, the creditors have called in their notes. You currently have 255 million credits outstanding on the Boundless. They want to take possession of it here at Plet station."

Falon started to say something, but Jason raised his hand to stop her. "Hold on a moment Falon." Jason turned back to Rogar. "What are the options?"

Rogar smiled at Falon, "There aren't many. The only way I see that you can pay this off is to sell all your patents. They've been trying for years to get them away from you anyway."

"They're my stable income. How am I going to keep all this going without the patent rights' percentages?"

"We make it work like it's suppose to," Falon interjected. She shrugged as if to say something more. "This is a freighter and we are suppose to haul freight for a living."

Rogar smiled, "We can bring suit against Delter for the liable contract that was signed and notarized through their offices. I calculate that we should be able to return the value of this ship after legal fees and maybe a little more."

Jason frowned, "They are not the ones to blame." He stopped as if weighing what he was saying.

Rogar looked from Jason to Falon, then said, "You can speak freely in front of me." His glance said that he wasn't sure about Falon.

She didn't miss the implication, "Piss off slime ball. Jason and I have crawled through some tough times together. He knows where I stand."

Jason nodded, "There was an Imperial Scout waiting for me in the asteroid belt. They tried to kill me."

Rogar nodded frowning, "I was afraid it was something like that. When I pressured the banks on the loan, the answers lent themselves to that interpretation." Rogar sat back thinking, "Then we have to sell the patents and before they become devalued."

Falon snorted, "How'd you come up with that one, slimer? You getting a commission on the sale?"

Rogar gave her a dirty look, "Yes, I will. However, it's really pretty simple. The government, the Empire, runs the patent office. They make the rules, they get to change the rules. All they need do is fabricate some instances of drive failure or whatever the item is, then get the patents reevaluated for safety. By their engineers, of course and all of a sudden the patents become worthless." He steepled his hands in front of his face. "But, if we sell now, we get to set the price. I know of two shipyards that would pay dearly for them. At least enough to cover the bank notes and probably half again as much more."

Jason rubbed his hands across his face, "You sure?"

"Jason, these are high stakes." Rogar turned dead serious, "Just like last time. I didn't realize just how big a grudge the admiralty would hold, but it's big. If they would try and kill you, then they certainly would try and financially ruin you. We must act quickly."

Falon shook her head, "Why are you listening to this guy?"

"I trust him."

"He's a lawyer, slime walking!!!"

"Look Ms.," Rogar paused as if going to use a different name, "Falon. Jason and I go back much further then you and he. I have his best interests in mind. He is my client."

Jason smiled, "I saved his life once, then gave him something that made him rich."

Rogar smiled grimly, "They've offered me quite a bit to drop your account. My firm is getting pressure as well. You had better keep your head down."

"This is the second time they've tried to kill me." Jason's face turned hard, "The first time was through the Civilization process. It was tampered with so that I would be slowly driven insane." Both Falon and Rogar looked at him with pity in their eyes.

"Do you have evidence?" Rogar's eyes were hard with anger.

"Nothing that you could use." Jason waved at him, "I'm better now. Go sell my patents. Do what you do best, rape them. Hurt them on Delter too." Jason got serious, "Don't let them drag you down with me. Jump clear if you have to."

Rogar got up to leave and grabbed Jason's shoulder on the way by him, "I will fight them to my last breath, and bleed them while making them think they like it. Good day, Ms. Falon."

Falon ignored Rogar as he left the galley. All her attention was on Jason. "You never told me that was how they Civilized you," a strange tone in her voice.

Jason looked at Falon with the pity in her eyes, "I don't want to talk about it." He got up and left the galley.

# XVI

"Jason," Falon announced over the com link. "Would you come to the bridge?"

Jason looked up from a microscopic examination of the alien artifact he'd recovered. "What's up?"

"What's the status of the refit?"

"We've completed the mini refit and restocked. Fred's been upgraded with additional piloting and navigational modules as well as more core memory." Jason put away his equipment while he talked. "She's space worthy and ready. It's time to find a cargo."

"Well, I've been working on that. Only it's harder than we thought. The Empire has been making inquiries about us, which makes potential customers nervous, and the cargoes available are too pat. Now Fred tells me that two Imperial warships just docked and they've been asking about us. We need to leave." Falon sounded tired and frustrated. Jason knew she was worried. He didn't know how he knew, but he knew.

"Okay," Jason tried to sound cheerful, "I'm on my way."

"Can we run empty to a better port?" Falon asked through the passageway speakers.

"No, the refit cost quite a bit. We need to make some credits."

Jason walked onto the bridge. "Fred, bring up the port cargo roster on the main screen." He turned to Falon and smiled as he sat down. She didn't smile back.

The main screen lit up with a multi-column listing of available cargo. Falon shook her head, "I've been all through it and I don't want to slant your opinion. Look it over and let me know what you think.

"Why don't you take a break? Get a cup of tea or whatever and let me look over your data."

Falon got up shaking her head mumbling as she left the bridge. She returned a few moments later with a cup of something warm.

Jason looked over the data and highlighted several possible candidates. Each one would've been fine, except each one was within half a percent of the Boundless's hold capacity and they all return a healthy profit. Jason sat back frowning, "You're right, this is all wrong. I've never seen even one cargo that matched our specs like these do, and there are six of them." Jason swung his chair to face his partner. "What are you thinking?"

Falon didn't hesitate, "It's a trap. The Empire wants you real bad, only they don't seem to want to follow their own laws. I don't get it." She let out an exasperated sigh as she sat down. "We'll have to trick them. Do something that's not in our normal operation. Like cargo, go high value or high risk, either way we get something quick and get a return on it. If what you tell me about their being able to get copies of our logs is true, then they know our set parameters for cargo as well. Our past record isn't that great for the high value cargoes"

"Why's that? I thought we were doing okay."

"Well," Falon hesitated cocking her head slightly, "let's just say that the principles weren't impressed by our crew. You having been Civilized and drunk in port most the time didn't send the message they wanted to receive."

"I wasn't drunk that much."

Falon shrugged but didn't comment. After a moment, she turned and started entering new parameters into the search routine. "Fred, try that and see what you get."

Jason stewed on the drunk in port comment. "*I didn't drink that much, did I*?" "Fred, what're our Imperial friends doing? Are they still trying to sap into your systems?"

"Yes, Jason they are still trying to interrogate outside of the shell we built. I think they suspect that we are not showing them everything. Falon, I think we have a match." The main screen changed slightly to highlight a cargo posting. Both Jason and Falon leaned in to study it.

"Not much mass to lift," Jason stated.

"It's got a perishable by date and," she whistled softly, "look at the return figures. We can make a profit on this one." She looked at Jason, "This is good and we can leave as soon as it's loaded." Jason was already indicating they would take it. Jason headed aft to act as supercargo, while Falon started filing the exit port documents. With luck, they would be in free space in two hours.

They loaded the cargo without a problem. Jason did notice several interested bystanders who should not have been on the dock. Once the cargo was secure, Falon expedited their departure. No one moved to stop them. And, because the cargo was a perishable, it didn't even look odd.

It took them two days to get out of the system to the jump point. There were a few ships in the area but nothing unusual. They jumped five more times without incident, each taking a day for calculation and hyperspace transit. The last jump was into the middle of nowhere.

"We have a beacon," Fred reported once the sensors had realigned and calibrated. "There are also five ships within sensor range. All of them appear to be Imperial warships."

Falon hit the intercom, "Jason to the bridge." She started calculating for a jump. "Fred, start emergency charging of the jump coils."

Jason arrived on the bridge out of breath. "What gives...." He stopped dead and looked at the main screen. "Shit! There are a lot of them. Fred, bring up the engineering console. Falon, stop calculating for jump and make contact for cargo delivery. Act like we have nothing to hide.

Falon shot a dirty look at him. He shrugged, "Okay, so we do have something to hide, but they may not know it. Communication is by fast courier ship and the ships run on a circuit, unless it's a scramble priority. Given the way they were acting about us, I don't think there is a general message out to apprehend us or they wouldn't have let us leave Plet. The cargo is legitimate and a rush delivery. Anyway, if they want us, they've got us. The jump coils have only started charging and will take 3 hours, if we reduce speed to half standard." Jason highlighted one of the ships on the viewer, "That is a ShHarzoid battleship. We can't outrun it, not to mention the four cruisers. Where are we?"

Falon let her breath out and slammed down a stylist, "This is listed as a deep space station, LPE2300. But it looks like an Imperial Navy depot of some type."

Jason smiled, "I think you're right."

Falon cocked her head toward him, "Why are you smiling?"

"Well, if this is a Navy depot, then whoever ordered this stuff is way, way up the food chain and is not going to question the prompt arrival. Also, they are probably not members of the Navy. They are probably a civilian administrator or more likely a contractor representative. This is pricey stuff. We are four days ahead of schedule."

"Jason, we are being hailed," Fred announced.

"Answer them," Jason and Falon said as one.

"They have requested our business here. I have responded with the cargo manifest, destination, and urgency." There was a pause. "They have accepted our credentials and I've been provided a flight plan." The holonav came on with a colored line representing their course shown. "This will take us to a private dock." There was another pause. Jason let his breath out.

"This isn't a trap," Falon said.

"I don't think so. We will drop this stuff and blast out of here as quick as possible."

"The Principle," Fred started again, "has a cargo to haul out of here. Are we interested?"

Jason and Falon looked at one another. Falon shrugged. Jason asked, "What are the conditions?" Both the pilot and engineer consoles displayed the particulars of the cargo. They studied them in silence.

"This cargo does meet our normal parameters of operation with a slight margin above normal profit," Fred smugly explained.

Jason shook his head, "Slight margin!! You've been working on your sarcasm program again. Sure we'll take it, as long as it can be loaded immediately. Tell him we have another commitment to make and no time to dally."

"Sent and received for. He agrees and the cargoes can be onloaded and offloaded simultaneously. He has noted our haste, based on the fact we are already charging for our next jump. He has added a bonus for prompt service."

"Docking in one hour fifteen minutes." Falon announced, "This one is going to be by the book." Jason just nodded.

# XVII

They had cleared dock and were into the first jump after the Navy depot, when Jason walked into the galley. Everything went off like clockwork. It had only taken seventy-two minutes to calculate for jump and everything was right the first time. The ship was running smoothly, Fred was in pilot mode, and there was nothing for the crew to do until they broke into real space again.

Falon was sitting at one of the tables, head leaning on the wall, staring into space. She had been jumpy and preoccupied during their entire stay at the Navy depot. They both had been concerned about being picked up by the Imperials, but it had been for nothing. Jason had to admit to himself, he had never paid much attention to her while in port. He normally dove into the first tavern and start pounding them down. But, he didn't think she usually acted like this. He noticed she had even done her hair differently. It was normally pulled back into a severe ponytail, now it hung loose about her shoulders. She was really good looking, red hair, green eyes, and pronounced cheekbones. Why hadn't he noticed before?

"Jason," she started, "I'm going to need to sell back my forty percent and move on."

Jason blew coffee all over the table, "What!"

She rotated her head while still resting it on the wall. "I don't want to get involved in this Imperial thing. I can't afford it." She took a deep breath and got up to get another cup of coffee and a rag. "I figure with what we've made on these two runs and the contingency fund, you can buy me out and I'll have about what I started with."

"But, but we're partners." He smiled weakly, "You know, I fix it. You fly it. You've always wanted a ship of your own. Ever since you got your license or at least that's what you've been telling me."

"I know this is sudden and I won't leave you without a pilot." Falon handed him the rag and sat down. "I just can't afford to compromise my license and position. If the Empire wanted to, they could ruin me without really trying. Flying is all I've got."

Jason felt like someone had just punched him in the stomach. "You've got forty percent of the Boundless." Falon's face was frozen into her "battle look". She never backed down when she looked like this. He nodded, "Okay, if that's what you want. I understand. We'll draw up the papers when we get to port." Falon didn't look too happy with her decision as she got up to leave. Jason wasn't thrilled either.

"Hey, ah," he waited for her to turn around, "ah thanks for a taking a care of me." Jason couldn't believe he was having trouble talking to her. "I ah, ah, well, thanks for being my partner. I hadn't realize just how much you had done."

Falon smiled, "No problem geek." She turned and left the galley.

They were into their second jump and settling into the standard procedure. Fred flew the ship and monitored all the systems, while Jason tinkered in his lab and Falon practiced her piloting skills in the simulator or worked out.

Falon was startled as Jason stepped out of the simulation room. He had converted one of the old crew spaces into a simulator room for Falon so that she could keep her flying skills sharp. She had never seen Jason use it. "So what gives?" she asked.

Jason looked up startled, "Huh, oh, hi. Just trying my hand. It's been a while and I thought I'd see if I still had it."

Falon smiled crookedly, "Did you ever have it?"

Jason swept the door open as he bowed and motioned her in, "Please step into my parlor and experience me flaming your ass."

Falon strutted by him, "That'll be the day."

# XVII

Four ship days later they were headed in system to drop their cargo and take on another one. Things were running smooth. "Fred, how long 'til docking?" Falon asked.

"Thirty-eight minutes at this speed. Traffic control has us locked onto beacon and I will be taking us in as planned."

Falon stretched, arching her back and throwing her arms wide. She was still wearing her sim-suit. It was skin tight so she could fit into the simulator seats, with a few probe cords hanging down. It left nothing to the imagination. She had lost track of the time and had to dash from the simulator room to the bridge. As she stood and turned she noticed Jason staring at her, "What's your problem?"

He blinked and looked back at his engineering display. "Just thinking which bar I was going to collect our bet in."

"Collect what? You owe me. I won that last battle."

"Do not. I took the one before and it was double or nothing."

Falon sighed, "I know how to settle this. Fred, what's our standing right now?"

"You hold the lead in small craft combat and one-on-one combat. Your skill in a fighter size craft seems to be of higher caliber than Jason's. However, he has you in squadron and destroyer conflict."

"That's cause he keeps cheating. Whoever thought about reshuffling the power grid and shutting down life support during battle."

"Actually, it was General Tontharkiel. He used it as standard battle practice."

Falon snorted, "Anyway, that's not what I wanted to know. Who's ahead in the betting? How much does he owe me?"

"You haven't been entering the actual betting so that I could track it, but based on your comments after the simulation events, Jason owes you a dinner out and you owe him a bottle of wine."

Falon smiled, "Sounds good to me. How 'bout you fly boy? Where you taking me?"

"Dressed like that, nowhere. I'd spend all evening beating off other guys."

Falon struck a seductive pose, "Since when have you cared?" She played with one of the probe cords.

Jason blinked a few times, "I guess you'er right. You can get pawed by anyone you like." He cleared his throat, "But I hardly think you'd want to be seen in the Hot Landing looking like that. All your pilot buddies would make fun of you."

"Hot Landing! They have one here?" For a moment, Falon looked like a little girl told about a dance. Then the diamond hard exterior came back, "You can't afford that."

Jason turned away to check a signal on his console. "Well, I figure it's the least I can do for a departing crew member." Silence descended with shocking speed. It was like they were both holding their breath.

"Yeah, right." Falon finally said, "I guess you're right. I'll go change. Fred, you have the Con."

"Aye, aye pilot Falon. I have the Con." Falon left the bridge very quickly. "Jason should I contact the legal company to have them start work on the contract change?"

Jason swung his chair around to look after Falon. Very softly he said, "Yeah, we should probably start doing that." He pulled himself back around to his console.

# XIX

Jason gingerly touched his lip and left eye. They both were really swollen. He looked at his reflection in the console monitor. It wasn't pretty. He didn't remember exactly how it started, but he did remember a fight, running from the shore patrol, and dodging their way back to the ship.

"We have permission to depart. Stand by to undock." Fred announced.

"I have the con," Falon slurred out while pulling herself upright in the pilot's chair.

"You are in no shape to pilot us out of dock, pilot Falon. My sensors indicate that your heart rate is elevated and body temperature low. You show every ind...."

"Shove it, Fred. I fly this thing."

"Not since signing the contract papers. You have no authority on this bridge." Fred responded smoothly.

Falon blinked a few times as if trying to focus her eyes. She brushed her hair back, and wiped her mouth on the back of her hand. "I haven't signed them yet. I still own forty percent. Now, I have the CON, chip head." She cracked her knuckles and wiggled her butt into the seat better. Her hands were rock steady as she put them on the controls.

"Jason, you are the Captain, what are your orders?"

Jason blinked, trying to get the blood out of his left eye. "Falon, you up to this?"

"Damn straight, twigit. I'm still breathing, I can fly this bucket."

"Do it, Fred. Give her the con. Notify port authority that we will be breaking seal in five minutes." Jason's hands, like Falon's, were rock steady as they flashed over the engineering panel, bringing all the systems on line. He knew the steps by heart, which was good since he couldn't focus on the switch names.

"Port Authority says all clear and clear skies."

"Falon, you awake?"

"Ah what, yeah. Time to fly." She struggled upright again.

"We have dock separation in five, four, three, two, one, now. Aft thrusters at 10 percent."

"We have dock separation. Distance increasing. Jason, the Port Authority is asking that we re-dock. They say there is some question about your and Falon's involvement in a riot at a local establishment."

"We are in space now. Tell them we don't know what they are talking about. Increasing forward side thrusters. Bring the nose about." Nothing happened. Jason looked over to see Falon slumped sideways in her chair with her arm hanging down. "Shit! Fred transfer all ships maneuvering control to my console and reconfigure for single flight control.

"I have complied. Your console is now configured for single operation. Jason, this is highly irregular. The Port Authority says you are backing too fast. They want you to heave to and stand by for tugs."

Jason pulled himself up straighter in the chair. "They haven't seen fast yet. Tell them to keep the tugs clear, I'm behind schedule." Jason's hands started flashing across the keyboard.

"Jason," Fred sounded concerned, "the thruster configuration is out of standard operation mode. Why are you initiating the main thrusters? We are too close to the spaceport. No, we aren't. We've cleared safe distance by seven meters. Jason, what...."

"Fred shut up! I'm having fun."

"What in all the hells of space," Falon sat up to see through the main viewing port, as the space port rotated by and below the nose of the ship. Another ship passed close aboard to starboard. Jason had rotated the ship vertically away from the docking port then pulled away in a clean reversing arch which left the station astern of them and below. The gravaton fields kept "down" in the same direction, but it didn't help the visual vertigo effects. "Oh shit," Falon gulped out as she covered her mouth and stumbled from the bridge.

"Jason, Falon is throwing up in the Captain's Underway cabin head. Shall I warm up the med unit? She appears to be inebriated."

"Not a bad idea. Have it warmed up and ready for both of us. Once we clear into free space I'll take her down there."

"Jason, one of the other freighters has sent a message to the pilot of this ship. They also are requesting the name of our pilot. How shall I respond?"

"Tell them and log the message so Falon can hear it later. Are we in free space yet?" Jason nudged the throttles up a hair.

"We will be in free space in seventeen minutes at this speed."

"I can't read the screen. Increase ship's speed to maximum allowed for this area of space and set a course for the jump point."

"Aye, aye Captain. Coming about."

# XX

Jason was in his shop tinkering with the alien artifact. He had been trying to piece together what had actually happened in the Hot Landing. He had been drinking and having a really pleasant time with Falon. She was good company. Then someone had joined them at the table. That's when it started getting fuzzy. Jason didn't like him and he had friends. Jason thought Falon knew them or at least knew about them. He couldn't remember. Shaking his head he reached for a tool and not finding it, he looked towards his tool caddy. Falon was sitting quietly on his workbench.

"Hi," she said.

Jason pushed back a little farther, "Hi, could you hand me a pico spanner with neutral tip?"

Falon gracefully hopped off the bench. She started on landing, and limped slightly as she walked over to the tool caddy, "Is that the purple one or the tan one?"

Jason smiled, "Tan."

Falon glanced over at Jason as she bent over the caddy, "Your face looks like shit. You got out of the med unit too early." She looked back at the tools trying to find the one he had asked for.

"No offense, but you don't look so great either. The cut over your eye is healing nicely. Another day and you won't be able to see the mark. And I've heard swollen pouty lips are all the rage." Falon pulled out a tool and walked over to him. "Not to mention your cat-like grace is a bit flawed." Jason noted her limping. "Hurt your ankle?"

Falon slapped the tool grip into his hand, "No, actually it's a fractured rib. It's healing. Tomorrow I won't feel it, five days from now, it'll be fine. Thanks, by the way."

"For what."

"For giving that ship my name as pilot. The maneuver you did leaving port impressed them and you let him think it was me." She rubbed at her side. "And after the fight and all, it will give my reputation a boost. You know," she lowered the pitch of her voice to imitate a man's, " If she can get the hell beat out of her and fly like that, well she's one hell of a pilot."

Jason smiled and turned back to the thing he was examining. "I don't remember how the fight started."

Falon snorted, "You hit a guy." Jason looked up at her. Falon was smiling in admiration. "It was a good punch too. Took him totally by surprise. Took him right off his feet, out cold, probably broke his jaw. You are suppose to be Civilized." Falon chuckled, "I started laughing, which pissed off his friends. They decided to teach the drunk, Civilized geek hero a lesson and," she stopped to brush her hair back, "well it got out of hand. There were several merchant marines in the place and they didn't take kindly to you getting pounded."

Jason sat back thinking hard, "The guy was groping you. That's why I hit him. He didn't think I would or," Jason thought harder. Something else was becoming clear, "or . . . or I hadn't in the past. You didn't like it, but weren't going to do anything about it." He turned his attention back to Falon, confusion written on his face.

"The guy was not groping me. I 'd've broken his arm if he touched me. He wanted to, he always wants to. But he wasn't. Is that why you hit him, to protect me?"

Jason cleared his throat, "Well a gentlemen does not treat a lady that way." He froze for moment, "Has this happened before?"

"A lady," Falon mused under her breath but wouldn't meet his eyes. "Yeah, its happened a time or two." She walked over to the artifact. "What's this thing do?"

Jason frowned. He knew her well enough to know that she wasn't going to give him any more data. He realized that there was a lot about her he didn't know. He felt bad, like he'd let some-one down, "I was too drunk to notice before wasn't I?" Jason hated himself right then.

Falon tapped the artifact with her finger, "Well? What's this thingy?"

"I don't know yet," Jason shrugged it off and bent down to a section of the exposed circuitry or whatever they were using to make it do what it did. "I was going to try and get this piece off and see it I could get power applied to it."

"Can I help?"

Jason was slightly amazed. Falon had never shown the least amount of interest in his tinkering in the lab. "Yeah, sure. Let's get you some protective clothing and gloves. I can raise the table up to ease the pressure on your rib. If you like." Falon gave him a look as she put on the indicated electrostatic free jump suit and gloves. "You know," he said with a smirk, "a change in perspective can be quite revealing."

Falon smiled through her cracked lips, "You talking about me or the artifact?"

Jason smiled and waved her over to the artifact without answering her question.

# XXI

Jason was tired. The last jump hadn't gone well. The six previous jumps hadn't been good either. They had dropped in too close to an uncharted heavy mass on the second jump out of Smith 259. It had pulled them off course and blew several overload breakers. The breakers were all in bad locations, hard to get to and awkward to work on. Falon had a terrible time calculating for jump because of the heavy gravitational fields in the area. It had taken her over nine hours to figure the vector to jump out of the hole. Every jump after that was a problem, hard to calculate and something broke. Sometimes it just worked out that way.

"Fred, where are we."

"We are three days out of Mixthol. Running in at all engines ahead standard. You seem tired Jason. Perhaps a sonic rub?"

Jason snorted, "Does it work? Everything else seems to have broken." He leaned his forehead against the bulkhead.

"Jason, you are exaggerating again. There have been several failures over the last seven days, but they are all within acceptable maintenance probabilities."

"You weren't the one running around fixing them. What's next on the list?"

"That was the last priority three job. The rest are 'fix as time allows'. We are due for a standard maintenance stand down. Four days in duration at an intermediate facility."

"Really, how much have we budgeted and do we have the credits?"

"Rounding up as you requested," Fred sounded miffed at the idea of not using the totally accurate figures, "we estimated this stand down at 400,000 credits with a margin of 100,000. You also have listed an update for me to add greater pilot independent reasoning and core capacity. We currently are showing a profit margin of 1.1 million credits. The current trend shows us earning 47 percent above the curve. If we get full value for this cargo, we will be another 100,000 ahead. So, after the stand down we should be 700,000 ahead. We are doing well. Does Falon really have to leave us? You two make a good team, economically speaking."

Jason pushed himself away from the wall, "It's her call. As far as I'm concerned she could stay with us forever."

"Have you told her that?"

"She knows. It's obvious."

"Jason, library entries indicate that the female of your species enjoys being told the obvious and often the male of your species doesn't do it enough. Also, what's obvious to one person is not always obvious to another."

Jason barked out a laugh, "I will agree with you on one thing."

"What is that."

"She is a female of my species." Jason laughed evilly, "Maybe she would like to take me on in another space battle."

"Falon is currently in the gymnasium working out."

"Really? How long she been there?"

"Fourteen minutes thirty eight decimal eight seconds."

"Fred, round up remember. Only computers and geeks talk in precise numbers." Jason picked up his tools and started off down the passageway. "I think I'll go work out as well. Ya never know, maybe I will catch her staring at my manly physique." Jason chuckled at the thought as he hurried down the passageway.

Jason dropped his tools, changed into workout clothes, and hurried to the gym. It was a standard model gym for a deep spacer. Space sailors had to be careful about exercise. Even with a gravaton field providing gravity, it was easy to lose muscle and tone.

Falon had the workout floor set at 1.1 gravities as she worked her way through several forms. She, as with most females, worked the martial forms with a mixture of gymnastics and martial arts, concentrating on speed, flexibility, and endurance. Even with genetic engineering and body sculpting, a woman's upper body strength didn't match that of a man's. Cybernetic implants could make a difference, but then they technically wouldn't be women anymore. Falon was strong and fast. Her body was in excellent condition, well toned, evenly proportioned, no bulk, streamlined, and she kept it that way. There was also no doubt that she was a fighter, a warrior. Jason admired that in her, as he had with all the Marines he had served with.

He stepped into the gym just as she completed a difficult double front kick, tuck roll foot sweep, spring to a middle stance with knife hand blow. She was dripping with sweat and her hand was a little low for the target throat area. Falon shook her head and brought her hand up to the right position, then stepped out of stance. "So geek, got it fixed yet?" She asked without malice.

"Yeah, for all the help you've been." Jason said with a smile.

Falon shot him a dazzling smile, "I fly it, YOU fix it. Fred, restore normal gravity."

"Normal gravity restored."

Jason started stretching his back and legs. "We will need to stand down for maintenance at Mixthol. There's an intermediate maintenance facility there that does okay work. It's going to be a little spendy, but worth it."

Falon frowned, "How spendy?"

"Well we're talking about half a million or so. Don't worry I will still have enough to buy you out and give you a profit." Jason changed to leg stretches while watching Falon cool down out of the corner of his eye.

Falon stopped and gave him an odd look, "Profit? How much profit? You just said this was going to cost half a mill."

"Well, we've done pretty good since Plet. So after we subtract off operating costs, restock and refit, and the maintenance, " Jason stopped stretching and smiled at her, "you'll get back your initial investment and an additional 280,000 credits."

"Jason, that's over my initial investment!" Falon was actually surprised. Her look turned hard, "Fred, is he telling me the truth? He's not cutting into his own funds is he?"

"No Falon, he's not giving you his share. The numbers he has reported to you are inaccurate in only that they have been rounded up. There are several assumptions which have been made as part of the calculations. If you would like I could provide you with the accurate figures and the assumptions. He did not include several upgrade costs to myself in these figures."

"You wouldn't get the pilot upgrade?"

"Not given these figures."

"Jason, we talked about that. You're going to need that upgrade without me around." Falon turned serious, "What about the memory, sensors pack, and the other stuff for you, Fred? Does this include that?"

"Falon, I don't need all that and we upgraded the pilot module on Plet," Jason said as he resumed stretching. "Fred and I will get along fine. I'm doing okay, now that I'm not Civilized anymore and we will be downside long enough on Mixthol to look for a good pilot and maybe a hand or two. Although," Jason stopped to look at Falon again, "I know I can't find anyone to replace you.

You are the best." He rolled over to do pushups and didn't notice the shocked look on Falon's face. "Fred, increase gravity to 1.2 in my area." He grunted.

"Gravity has been increased. No, Falon, the numbers provided to you did not include any of my discussed upgrades."

"Fred." Falon had to clear her throat, "add the upgrades to your maintenance invoice." Falon got to her feet frowning, "I'm going to go shower then check our course in system. Fred gets his upgrades." She stalked out of gym.

Jason was puzzled by her reaction. He'd thought she would be happier about the increased profit. Instead she wanted to buy Fred upgrades. He shook his head and went on exercising.

# XXII

Jason stepped out of the yard superintendent's office more confused than ever. The ship repairs had cost less than they estimated, but the bill had been much higher. Jason had even done some high value repair work on another ship to offset the cost of his own ship refit. Yet the bill had still been almost 300,000 more then he expected. The reason had been a simple one after the smiling and cheerful yardmaster had explained it. Falon had ordered several expensive upgrades to Fred. Not just piloting, but also auto-navigation, updated star charts, complete holonav suite upgrade, and, to top it all off an automated engineering assistant, complete with grav lifter and tool caddy. The Yardmaster assured him that he gave her a big discount on the engineering assistant because they were such good customers.

Jason smiled as he hurried through the yard. The outbound cargo should be loading and the new crewmembers reporting aboard. He was disturbed by the idea of new crew, but there was nothing to be done. Falon had packed up all her stuff and moved off the ship three days ago. He was amazed at how little she had. Of course, he didn't remember her reporting aboard at all. He had been drunk at the time.

He palmed his hand unit, "Fred, is the cargo and crew aboard?"

"Yes, Jason. Did you find the answer to your mystery?"

"Yeah, it was Falon. She authorized all the expenditures. Apparently the letter of ownership for the Boundless hasn't cleared the system yet. She's still listed as part owner. File for departure and we will lift ship as soon as I'm back aboard."

"Aye, aye Jason. Standing by for your return."

Jason put the hand unit away and quickly made his way back. The gantries and lifters were pulled back and away from the Boundless. She was resting on her landing legs looking eager to rise into space. Jason frowned as he noticed that the engines were cycling and ready for power. Jason palmed the airlock door open and hurried through the ship. As he arrived in the galley, he felt the vibration increase and the noise build.

"Fred, what in all the hells is going on. I didn't give the order to lift ship."

"Jason," Falon's voice spilled out of the speaker, "I'll explain it all to you when you reach the bridge."

Jason stopped, stunned, then broke into a run to the bridge.

Falon was in her normal seat, studying the traffic patterns of spacers on the screen. They had cleared atmosphere and were heading out. "Fred, maintain course and speed until we clear local space, then go to maximum permissible." She rose stretching from her pilot's chair, emphasizing her athletic form. Jason stopped at the sight of her. She turned around to see him standing there, "What's your problem?"

Jason leaned against the doorway, trying to act nonchalant, "Well, I'm rather surprised to see you. I thought you were pretty much gone from my ship and out of my life." He gestured with one hand, "But here you stand. What are you doing here?"

Falon shrugged out of her flight jacket and hung it on the back of one of the bridge chairs, "There was an Imperial survey ship through here about five days ago. They were asking a great number of questions about asteroid reefs in this district and the outside of Delter got mentioned. Then yesterday a courier ship spaced in. This place hasn't seen an Imperial ship in years. Now two in less than a week, it made me wonder. So I started asking around about the two guys you hired. The word under the street is that these guys only arrived five days ago."

"Coincidence?" Jason asked.

"I don't know." Falon shrugged, "but it felt odd."

Jason pushed himself away from the wall, "Thanks for the info, but why are you here? This is just going to get you tangled up in my troubles."

Falon quickly looked away, "Well, you were right about me wanting a ship. I started thinking about it after I left and realized I would probably never get another chance like this." She reached out to stroke the back of the pilot chair and turned her back to Jason. "The Boundless is a one of a kind, between Fred and you," her voice drifted to silence.

Jason smiled from ear to ear. He could barely contain his excitement as he stepped forward. He reached out and tapped her on the shoulder. When she turned to face him, he put his hand out asking for a handshake. "Like I said before, you can stay as long as you want, forever if you want."

She took his hand, "You never told me that." She gave him a wry smile, "You certainly replaced me fast enough."

"I only hired a pilot. I could never replace you." Their eyes met and both of them froze holding hands. Jason started, dropping her hand he turned away, "Ah, ah, I built you your own Simulator, that should've been message enough. Ya know I wouldn't do that for just any old pilot."

Falon smiled softly at his back, "Yeah that's right. Pilot scum shouldn't go any further aft than frame 168, the galley." She put some sting into her voice as she repeated one of the age-old antagonisms between engineering and deck officers.

Jason laughed, "That's right and don't you forget it." He turned back to her, trying to look serious, "You know, buying back your forty percent is going to cost more. We are making a profit now."

Fire rekindled in Falon's eyes, "Think so?" she swiped the jacket off the chair and shoved her hand in a pocket, while stalking toward him. She stopped centimeters from his face, and raised her hand up so she could sprinkle torn pieces of paper in the air in front of his nose. "I never signed it. So forty percent is still mine. I want to see the books. If we're making a profit, I want my share."

Jason huffed and turned to walk off the bridge. "You spent your share on an automated engineering assistant. Thanks, by the way," he said as he went through the hatch.

Falon threw her jacket after him. Then she wistfully made her way back to the pilot seat. She wiggled in pulling her feet up under her with a very satisfied look on her face.

"Do you want me to display the financial data for your review?" Fred asked.

"No."

"But you just told Jason that..."

Falon chuckled, "I did, didn't I." She unfolded her legs and grabbed the controls. "I have the Con. Fred, put some music on. I'll fly her for awhile."

# XXIII

"Okay here's the plan," Jason and Falon were huddled around a table in the galley loaded with charts and graphs. "We will drop into real space in about two hours. We should come in about a day out from the asteroid reef." He reached over and pulled a chart out. "Here's where we were when the Shard jumped us. Given the drift of the wreckage, time, and speed of drift," his finger traced down a line drawn on the chart to a large red circle, "this is the probable area that it would have drifted into. I have calculated the error factor of probable deflection based on estimated micro meteor strikes and known gravitational activities in the area. I then added an error factor for the unknowns. So, this circle represents the most probable area of search for the Shard," His finger traced the large red circle. "With a survey ship somewhere near here, I don't want to go banging around with the beacon activation strobe on. So, I think we should get into the area, then do limited duration activation, LDA. When we get a beacon active signal we will send out the shut down code and hightail it to the salvage."

"Why wouldn't the survey ship already have picked up the salvage?"

"They may have, but not from our beacon. I have ours coded so that they will only transmit when they receive a special signal.

Hopefully, only from us." Jason leaned back, "This is a big reef. There are millions of bits of rocks, minerals, and metals floating around in there. The odds are on our side. Without a point of search to start from, they could be searching a long, long time."

"Doesn't that apply to us and this asteroid of yours?"

Jason stopped smiling, "I hope not. We set beacons on nearby asteroids. I'm hoping," he leaned up and pulled another chart from the pile to put it on top, "that we can retrace our course through the reef." His finger traced another line to a large blue X, "When we reach here and transmit we should get some type of response."

Falon snorted, "Like an Imperial scout de-ghosting to take a shot at us."

"Ah, no! I'm hoping one of the beacons gives us a return. That will allow us to relocate the tech facility." He leaned back again, taking a drink, "Then the fun really begins."

Falon frowned at him. She didn't like him drinking and he knew it. "You haven't been able to figure out the thing we have now. So what are you going to do with a whole hangar?"

"I'm hoping to find an educator," Jason held up his hand at Falon's look. "This appeared to be a fairly large and complete facility. There were over a dozen vessels on the pad and other openings that appeared to be doors leading further into the hillside. Now, given the obvious superior tech level, they should've solved the automated education problem. With an educator, I can learn some of the tech and hopefully repair one of the ships."

"Jason, you're hoping they solved the problem? What are we doing out here?" Falon turned away raising her arms to the ceiling in an imploring gesture.

"The Empire is very close to solving the problem. There are several instances of prototype devices having partial success. Given the sophistication of their technology, this is a logical problem for them to have tackled." Jason sighed and looked down at the charts. "If there isn't any education equipment, then we will stake a claim and sell the rights of exploration to the Empire for a tidy amount." He took another drink.

"The Empire," Falon echoed in disbelief. "This would be the same Empire that had you Civilized, which you aren't anymore. The same Empire that sent a Splinter class scout ship out to kill you."

"Well, I've been thinking about that. We could go public with our find first. That should make it difficult for the Navy or PsySec to take any action. There is LAW after all. They are sworn to uphold it."

Falon gave him an odd look. "Those who make the laws, can remake the laws," she quoted. "Some jerk told us that. Weren't you listening to him?" Falon swung back toward him and speared him with a finger to the chest. "I tell you what, I'm hoping we find some good stuff we can sell for lots and lots of credits, so we can run and hide for a while. I know a few places where the Empire doesn't control."

Jason blinked a few times in confusion, "You do. Where?"

Falon looked daggers at him, "Okay, I've never been to any of these places." She paused to recompose herself, "There's Paladin, Trader's Rock, Convection 291, and a few others."

"Those are all pirate legends!"

"Not legends. I flew with a guy that knows how to get out of Imperial space."

Jason looked skeptical, "Yeah, sure he does."

Falon looked like she wanted to hit him as she stood. "I'm going to work out. See you on the bridge in two hours. Sober!"

Jason put his drink down and smiled at Falon's departing back. He was drinking fruit juice.

# XXIV

"So what do we do now?" Falon asked looking clear eyed and sharp as a razor.

"We keep searching."

"It's been four days since we started back tracking and we haven't gotten a nibble."

"Falon, this may take some time. The asteroid may have drifted away. The beacons may have gotten smashed. There are a lot of possibilities."

"How long are we going to search before we call this off?"

Jason frowned and turned from his engineering console to look at her again. This time he swiveled his chair around. "What's wrong?"

Falon was taken back, "What are you talking about? Nothing's wrong. I was just curious."

Jason smiled; he had been paying a lot more attention to Falon since Plet and was starting to understand her ways. "You've asked me these same questions four times in the last two days. Now, what's got you bothered?"

Falon looked back at him with the diamond exterior in place. Jason was learning to read that too.

"Okay, I'll guess." Jason said with a smile, "We have recorded an unusually high level of ion residue in the area, could be the survey ship. We picked up several cubic meters of outstanding salvage from the INS Shard. Let's see: we got a missile launcher, a turret, fire control system and magazine, fully intact, a secondary computer completely intact, a sensor ghosting projector, a cannon, a fusion torroid for fuel preparations, several hundred feet of gravaton transmission grid, and every precious metal and rare earth material. Fred, what did we estimate the worth at?"

"Rounding up, approximately 44 million credits."

"That alone would pay for us staying in this reef for about a year at our current consumption rate, but it looks funny. All of it is Imperial standard equipment for a spy ship. The ghost module alone would guarantee we visit a detention area. So that probably has you bothered." Jason squinted at her, "Probably the other ship in the area too?"

Falon gave him a dirty look. "It doesn't feel right," she stated with some conviction. "It all doesn't feel right. The longer we stay out here, the more I think this is a bad idea. If the asteroid was where you said it was, we should've found it yesterday."

"That's part of the salvage trade. Sometimes we have to look around a bit."

"This morning you said you received a long-range sensor probe from an Imperial ship, probably the survey ship."

"Don't worry about the Imperial. We can detect them at twice the range they can find us using those type of active sensors."

"Jason, we are risking the Boundless."

Jason smiled, "I thought you liked flying her through the reef?"

Falon nodded, "I do, but that doesn't change the fact that if I screw up, we hit or get hit by a chunk of rock. As you found out before, if it's moving fast enough, blotto, we're so much junk. The shields are already deflecting a great deal of debris. This reef is a ship killer. All the navigation charts have warnings about it. You were nuts to try it the first time."

"I can't argue that. Let's give it another day or two. If we can't come up with something by then, we will pull out for some rest and relaxation. Okay?"

Falon looked resigned, "Okay." She turned back to her controls, "This will be worth a lot of credits, right?"

"We find this place and we will be able to write our own ticket, even with the Empire. This is lost technology, I'm sure." Jason studied his console a moment. "Let's come over about ten degrees and move about three light seconds."

"Aye, aye. I'm bringing her around slowly. Ahead point 2."

They flew on for several hours, making minor course adjustments. Jason was taking them closer to the larger asteroids. It was boring and dangerous. At least half a dozen times, Falon had to use their small fusion cannon to either redirect or vaporize incoming meteorites.

Fred sounded excited as he announced. "Jason, I have a match."

"Where away?"

A three-dimensional image rose up in the holonav. It showed a large asteroid nestled in close to three others. At a distance it looked like one really big one, but was really four packed closely together.

Jason hurriedly compiled, reviewed the data, and then cross-correlated it to the previously compiled data on the asteroid. "That's it! Fred's right!!" He calculated several things simultaneously, "Okay Falon, let's go into orbit, but not too close. Last time it tried to pull us down." He gestured to the holonav, "Here's the course to orbit and the orbit calculations. You're going to have to stay on top of it all the time because of the shifting gravities."

Falon sighed, "Jason, go figure your approach out and leave the ship piloting to me."

Jason stopped for a moment, "Right. I'll go ready the Tigerous and the equipment I need." He all but ran from the bridge.

"Fred, keep a close watch on him. As excited as he is, he could do something stupid."

"As you wish, Falon. He does seem to be very active."

# XXV

Jason spent several hours finalizing his equipment and making sure it was working. He moved several items to the Tigerous that were not a part of her normal equipment complement. The Tigerous herself was a space station service tug that Jason had modified, adding manipulator arms, exterior articulated tools, gravity lock fields, and towing mounts. She was housed in a service bay in the lower forward part of the Boundless's hull. The service doors were under the bridge and there was a service way that went aft from the service bay to the forward holds on both the port and starboard side. That way, the Tigerous could bring back salvage, dock, and then would be off loaded with the salvage stored in one of the forward holds. She looked like a wingless fly with spider like pinchers on the face. She weighed in at about 150 metric tons and had everything except a jump drive to make her spaceworthy.

"Falon, how does it look in orbit? Any debris nearby?"

"I've established a stable orbit as far away from the asteroid as I can get and still be in orbit. There is nothing really threatening nearby at this time. Why?"

"Jason is going to move his assault armor forward by walking the exterior of the ship. The armor is rather cumbersome and he might damage something by moving through the interior passageways."

"Fred, what are you talking about? Assault armor? Jason, what are you doing with a set of assault armor?" Assault armor was the Imperial answer to personal space armor. It was powered armor with communication equipment, grav drive, navigation gear, and weapons mounted on several hard points. It would give an infantryman the strength of an earthmover and the firepower of a reinforced platoon of marines.

"I acquired a set when I worked in the shipyard and had it modified to add tools and instruments. It's like a heavily armored version of a tool suit. It's been really handy." Jason grunted, "Sorry, I stepped kind of hard on the deck. Anyway, I remounted the needler turrets on the shoulder points, and put the normal combat lasers back into the arm mounts. I should be able to handle about anything wearing this, if I have to get out of the Tigerous."

Falon frowned, "Fred, turn on external cargo camera four, and focus on our boy wonder." One of the smaller bridge cargo-loading monitors came on and an image of a metal man with pronounced shoulder boards and several bulges and spikes walking on the outside of the ship came into focus. He was bright violet, standard Imperial engineering color, with dull gray shoulder boards and forearms. She watched as Jason gracefully walked up the length of the ship.

"Fred, cycle cargo lock two and standby to bring me on board."

"Aye, aye sir."

Jason grabbed the edges of the lock with his hands and kicked his legs out to swing into the lock. It was poetry in motion. "Fred, cycle the lock shut and stabilize the atmosphere."

"Aye, aye sir. Lock shut and atmosphere stabilizing."

"Fred, where's the engineering assistant?"

"It is located outside of your shop, in stand by."

"Well get it up here. I'm ready to load and commence final check."

"Fred, take the Con. I'm going to Tigerous service bay." Falon launched herself out of the pilot chair and hurried off the bridge. She continued to hurry through the ship, then stopped several meters from the service bay, and stood still until the engineering assistant floated by. Slowly, almost reluctantly she allowed the floating assistant to draw her forward into the bay.

Jason was walking down the aft loading ramp on the Tigerous, "Good, it's here. Ginger, store it away in cargo slot eight then synchronize with Fred for navigation and communications."

Ginger was the onboard computer for the Tigerous. "Aye, aye captain," it's voice was much more computer like than Fred's.

"Hi Falon, I thought you were suppose to be on the bridge. You know, dangerous asteroid reef, pilot's place is at the helm, and all that."

"Yeah, well I thought I would come down, see you off, and tell you to be careful. There's only the two of us out here." She abruptly turned away from him and walked up into the Tigerous.

Jason followed her cautiously up the ramp. She was acting odd again. "You didn't have to come all the way down here for that." He looked around trying to figure out what she was here looking for.

Falon was standing in front of his assault armor. "How much damage will this take?"

"It a quarter inch of battle steel reinforced by standard shield fields. Specs say it will take the sustained output of a needler semi-portable cannon. The energy dissipaters can shunt everything up to a secondary fusion cannon. I don't think I would trust it that far." Jason's confused look cleared, "Don't worry, I'll be careful."

Falon reached out to run her hand across the armor plate covering the thigh of the assualt armor. "Orbital imagery has matched up. I've fed the coordinates of the previous landing site to Ginger. She can take you down to exactly where you were before."

"Jason, Falon, the check list has been completed and all items accounted for. Ginger reports that the Tigerous is ready for launch."

"Okay Fred. Everything's ready."

Falon stepped forward and gently kissed him on the cheek, "Good luck." She turned and hurried from the service bay.

Jason stood rooted in place, shifting his eyes from side to side. "Fred, did you record what just happened?"

"No, Jason. You and Falon were standing in the Tigerous' cargo bay. I have no cameras or sensors in there."

Jason shook his head and closed the cargo ramp on the Tigerous. "Okay Ginger start cycling the engines. Bring all navigation systems online. We're going a salvaging." He moved up to the cockpit and strapped himself in.

"All systems ready for launch."

"Ginger, contact Fred and tell him to start launch sequence."

Fred's voice came through the headset. "Service bay is evacuated. Standby for door sequence." Jason watched the doors open to space. "Good luck, Jason. No debris in the launch window, graviton field has been neutralized, and you are ready for launch."

Jason grabbed the controls as he felt himself go weightless. Then he eased the Tigerous off her legs as the automatic tie downs released and forward out of the service bay. Falon's voice came through, "You are in free space, Tigerous."

"I copy Boundless. Going to standard drive." Jason pushed the Tigerous away from the service bay, noticing that the doors were already closing. He circled over the top of the Boundless and started toward the surface of the asteroid.

The trip down was uneventful but stressful. He was ready to pull up and run at a second's notice. Nothing happened. Using the visual imagery and navigational directions provided by the Boundless, he located the canyon and came in to hover near the left-hand wall. He could still see the depression in the dirt that the Boundless's landing skids had made. Without hesitation, Jason eased the nose over to the seeming rock wall and started cutting a hole in with the forward salvage torch. The rock wall didn't want to cut nor did it act like rock. Jason eased back a bit and fired the forward plasma cannon. It punched a nice hole in the wall. Jason fired it a few more times, widening the hole until the Tigerous could fit inside.

"Boundless, this is Tigerous."

"Okay, Jason, we still have you on sensors."

"I've blown a hole into the hangar and I'm about to enter. Last time, I lost communications. So don't panic. I'm going to go in and pick up something and come right out. No more then fifteen minutes."

"I copy Jason."

"Here I go." Jason eased through the hole.

The cavernous space dwarfed the Tigerous. The Boundless could easily have fit into the space. It was just as Jason remembered it, a dozen or so ships of various sizes evenly spaced across the surface. Jason eased over to one of the smaller ones and picked it up with the towing locks. He slowly turned the Tigerous about and headed back through the hole. Once out, he went to full thrust.

"Did you lose telemetry?"

"Yes, we did. You disappeared from everything, sensors, communications, everything."

"Okay. I'm in bound with a small ship in tow. Open hold five and standby to receive cargo."

"Okay. Hold is open and we are standing by."

Four hours later, Jason was sitting in the galley drinking coffee and trying to focus his eyes. "Got a clue?" Falon asked.

"Not a one." He tiredly sipped at the coffee. "I've tried everything I can think of and can't even get it open. I'm not even sure where the hatch is, if it has one." Jason got up and walked over to the drink dispenser. "I'm going to have to go back and explore around."

Falon slapped him on the back, "Get some sleep first. Then we'll plan a mission. I've got Fred looking into communications methods."

"Yeah, okay." Jason trundled off to his stateroom.

Six hours of sleep made him feel like a new man. He met Falon in the galley. "So Geek, how you feeling?"

"I'm okay. Sleep was a good idea."

"Thank Fred."

"Thanks Fred. What have you come up with on communications?"

"I propose you use an optic link through the hangar opening to a relay station located on the surface."

Jason nodded, "That's a good idea, Fred. I think Cryton is already rigged with a relay transmitter and an optical receiver."

"My records indicate that you are correct. I will have Cryton power up, undock and proceed to the asteroids surface."

"Sounds good, Fred. Make it so."

"I think I should go down with you." Falon held up her hand to forestall his comment. "I can stay in the Tigerous while you are out walking in your suit. Perhaps if I'm in the hangar with you I can monitor your progress inside and relay to Fred."

"I need you up here."

"Why? There's nothing going on. Fred can handle shooting any meteors that get too close and limited course adjustment. I'm not doing anything."

Jason thought a moment, "Okay, you in the Tigerous wearing a utility suit. Me in my assualt armor. Okay, we can make this work." Falon nodded and rushed off to get changed. Jason went to the service bay to preflight check the Tigerous. This all felt wrong somehow, but he couldn't put a finger on what.

Falon showed up just as preflight was completed. He and Falon boarded and proceeded to launch. Everything went like clockwork.

The hole Jason had blasted in the wall was still just as he had left it. Falon carefully moved into the hanger and set the Tigerous down behind the line of ships, closer to the back wall of the hangar. Once landed, Jason quickly set up the optical linkage between the Tigerous, Cryton, and the Boundless.

"Fred you on line?"

"I am standing by Jason. All systems are normal. Do you want me to report all course corrections and anti meteor-activity?"

"Only if you calculate that it will potentially endanger the ship."

"Aye, aye sir."

"Jason I see a doorway," Falon said. "I will illuminate it with the forward spotlight. Currently I measure point three gravities in this hangar. That's point one five Gs higher than outside."

Jason moved over to it using his grav unit. After inspecting it for a moment he said, "I can't see anyway to open it, so I'm going to smash it open." So saying Jason pushed on it. The assualt armor's superior strength proved more then the door could handle, it crumpled in, revealing a passageway. Jason studied the opening.

"I'm getting a sensor echo from beyond the door. It appears to go straight for several hundred meters. There are multiple openings off the passageway. Jason, this place is huge."

"It looks large enough for me to move around in the suit. I'm going in for a quick look." He stepped through the doorway and carefully moved down the passageway, pausing to record and observe along the way. He moved from room to room, slowly recording and analyzing what he was seeing as best he could. The culture and technology was alien, but the aliens seemed to be humanoid in structure, based on the furniture and other items they uncovered. It was fascinating.

"Jason, how long can that armor support you? You've been at it for twelve hours."

"Assualt armor can provide life support for about eight days, but it's no fun after about three. I'm not planning on being in here that long. Give me another five hours, then I'll come out."

"Okay. The link is holding to Fred. I'm sending all this info to him."

"Ya know Falon, I'm not seeing any indication of power. There are no lights, no heat sources, no indications that energy is flowing anywhere that my sensors can detect."

"Jason, I don't like it again. Something feels wrong. Would you come back to the ship please?"

"What, again?" Jason took a deep breath. "Let me check this next room out and I'll come back. I need to get out and stretch anyway." Jason stepped into a room filled with clutter and benches. He froze in the doorway, there was something familiar about the arrangement. "Falon, you've been mapping the topology of these rooms right?"

"Yeah, I've got a map."

"Where is this room in relation to the hanger?"

"It should be just on the other side the wall."

"I'm going to step out of this room. See if you can burn a hole into here with a torch."

"I'm too far away to use the torch, and I'm not going to fire the cannon."

"Okay, I'll punch a hole from this side." Jason sounded frustrated as he stepped over to the wall. This room was fairly large with what looked like overhead track ways. As Jason got closer, the wall slid into the floor revealing the hanger and Tigerous on the other side. The plasma cannon swiveled around to point at the room. Jason froze.

"Did you do that?" Falon asked nervously.

"I think so." Jason bent down as far as the suit allowed, examining the floor. "There is some type of crystal inlay here. It must be a switch or proximity indicator." He straightened up. "I think this is a maintenance shop. It looks like tools and benches. One of these things looks exactly like the one I've been tinkering with."

"Jason, we are losing power." Falon reported, "It's only about a two percent loss, but I can't trace the point of loss."

"Make preparations to get underway. Fred, what do your sensors show?"

"Nothing Jason. Everything is normal."

"I'm returning to the Tigerous." Jason took a bounding step towards the open portal and it slid shut. "Shit! I'm going to punch a hole." He raised his right arm and fired the laser rifle.

The beam impacted the wall and might as well have been a spot light. "Nothing with lasers, switching to needlers." Shoulder turrets came to life and sparks flew when the needle rounds hit the wall. "I'm going to come out the long way. I don't understand, the metal wasn't that tough a moment ago." He spun around and started moving toward the passageway.

"Jason, power lose has risen to ten percent," Falon reported, "and we've lost communications with the Boundless. I'm going to burn a hole from my side. Get out of the way."

"I'm clear of the door." Jason paused then added, "something moved in here."

Falon could hear the excitement in his voice. She grabbed the fire control grip for the plasma cannon, aimed at the top edge of where the door had been and let go with a burst of energy. It splashed against the wall, scarring it but not making a hole. She shot again. This time she got a hole.

"Shplenic varth traplan. Vistarn hiesiplark!" sounded through the speakers.

"That sounds awful familiar, " Jason turned away from the glowing hole in the wall. Across the space from him was a violet, glowing, many-armed figure. It was coming towards him. "Falon, abort and return to the Boundless. I will try to get to the surface for pick up. I repeat abort." He turned the armor on full and started blasting away with both turrets and lasers, as he backed towards the wall.

"I'm not going to leave you here." She started cycling main engines and unlimbered the forward cargo arms. When systems reported ready, she lifted the Tigerous and moved it closer to the wall. Both salvage torches ignited, they were a thousand times hotter than a sun. Sparks flew as she started cutting the wall away. She was cutting, and peeling, hoping and praying that Jason's armor would protect him from the radiation.

"Power levels dropping," Ginger's computer voice reported, "Power less than sixty percent."

The wall collapsed outward with a pull from a thruster. Jason, still struggling in his assualt armor, was being hauled feet first out of the opposite doorway by some type of gravity field. Communications had been lost. Falon slammed the controls forward trying to grab him with the port cargo arm. The Tigerous crashed into the upper edge of the door and stuck. Jason disappeared through the door scant meters from the arm. In frustration, Falon slammed the thrusters in full reverse and backed the Tigerous out of the hole. She spun the tug around, end for end, shifting the thrusters to give it a fluid graceful flight, as she started toward the now closing opening out of the hangar. She retracted the landing skids and extended the arms straight out to provide the smallest possible cross section for the tug and shot through the opening. Once into free space, she went to full power and rocketed away from the surface.

"Fred, start emergency docking procedures. I am inbound and losing power."

"I copy Falon. Emergency procedures have been initiated. I detect no power loss."

"We'll figure it out later. Jason has been captured or taken by something in the asteroid. What kind of weapons do we have on board? Is there another set of assault armor? Something I could fit into."

"We have a full complement of hand weapons as specified by interstellar commerce regulation and a few others that Jason acquired. There is no other set of assault armor on board. Jason did have plans for installing several cannons on the Tigerous."

"Pull them out. I'm two minutes from docking." Falon made a no nonsense approach and docked the Tigerous in record time.

"Okay Fred, how can we find Jason?" she asked while stepping down from the Tigerous' ramp.

"I don't know. There seems to be some type of sensor suppression going on. I am not familiar with a technology that can do that."

"Fred, damn it," Falon slammed her hand down on the service bay engineering console, "We need some type of answer. Jason has been taken. I'm not the engineering genius he is, but I do know how this ship works. There has to be something we CAN do!!"

"Falon, I understand your concern, but I don't have the capabilities needed to give you answers. Nor is this technology something within Imperial standards. We are dealing with an alien culture. Logic would dictate that we leave orbit and try to find help."

Falon banged her hands on the console speaker, "I don't want logic! I want Jason back!" she yelled at Fred. "Bring up the plans for the modification to Tigerous. Have the engineering assistant powered up and report to me." She looked around suddenly, "Where's Cryton?"

"I lost contact with it on the asteroid. No information available."

Falon took a deep steadying breath, "Okay," she set down at the engineering console to study Jason's modification plans. "Fred, power up Stix and have it haul the weapons forward to the service bay."

"Stix is in motion. You will have to leave the bay for depressurization. The main service bay doors will have to be used."

"Very well, I will be on the bridge." Falon spent the next several hours on the bridge pouring over engineering plans and drawing. She was very thankful for the engineering assistant. It had the basics of engineering, metallurgy, welding and joining techniques, electronics, optoelectronics, and all the other skills needed to make these kinds of modifications. All she had to do was tell it what she wanted done and it would do the work. It still was hard work.

Stix moved the weapons pieces to the service bay. Falon, and the sturdy, tireless assistant, turned them into weapon systems. It was going to take days to make all the changes, but she had a plan.

"Falon, we are losing power. There has been a ten-percent loss in power output from the main power units. Calculations indicate that we are under attack. What should I do?"

"What? How should I know?" She composed herself with another deep cleansing breath. "What is the trend of the power loss? And why do you think this is an attack?"

"The power loss has had a steady positive trend over the last hour, just now reaching ten-percent of total generator outputs. This is consistent with our last landing on the asteroid. That is why I calculate that we are under attack."

"What did Jason do last time?" Falon moved over to the engineering console in the service bay.

"He lifted ship from the asteroid and went to main engines to escape the graviton capture beam."

"They have a graviton capture beam, like what a tug would use?"

"Yes, only the range was much greater."

Falon had a bad feeling and started racing for the bridge. "What kind of range?"

The Boundless shuddered, nearly knocking Falon off her feet. "The range would not be sufficient to lock on to us in this orbit.

Our power loss has risen to thirty-percent and our forward velocity has slowed by one half."

"Fred, you idiot, we have just been grabbed by that beam thing. Why didn't you tell me they could do this?"

"I didn't know they had this capability. When last we were here, the beam stopped functioning much closer to the asteroid's surface. We are losing altitude."

Falon's hands flashed over the panel and she eased the main drive throttles forward. The Boundless shuddered, bucked and slowly started pulling away.

"Power loss now to fifty-percent and engine efficiency is down by thirty-percent. Mass sensors indicate there is something astern of us." Fred reported impassionately.

"Bring up number four engine camera. Increasing speed to ahead one third. Standby to help evade when we snap free."

"Camera online. Standing by to lend assistance."

The aft looking camera provided a view of a blue glowing funnel catching the ion exhaust and channeling it down toward the asteroid. "What in all the hells of space is that?" She studied it a moment, then pushed the throttles ahead full. The Boundless bucked wildly.

"Engine efficiency is down seventy-percent. We are losing altitude. Impact, at current rate of descent, in ten minutes thirty-eight seconds. Engine temperatures are rising. Forward strain gauges are showing hull strain at eighty percent of rated levels. Data would indicate that the capture field has us locked just forward of amidships, while the aft structure is capturing our thrust exhaust."

Falon was very calm, "Fred, calculate our point of touchdown and display it on the holonav." She turned to look at the three dimensional model of the asteroid to see where they were going to crash. A red dot appeared.

"Falon, our point of impact coincides with the location of the structure you and Jason explored."

"Fred, we aren't going to crash. We are going to be forcibly docked. The same thing that got Jason has us, now."

# XXVI

"*What was I drinking*?" Jason felt terrible. He dimly became aware of metal underneath his bare back and butt. He was cold, wet, and naked. Struggling to move, he groaned from the pain in his head, neck, chest and groin.

"Come on, Jason," something hit him in the face. "Come on, wake up. You can do it. We gotta get moving."

"*Move! You've got to be kidding*," he thought to himself. He coughed, and the world started to fade.

Warm hands started pushing on his chest and rubbing his arms. "Come on. Don't leave me. We have to get you out of here."

He liked the hands rubbing him. If only they didn't feel worried, afraid, and desperate. He pried his eyes open to look at blurry, flickering lights. He groaned and shut them again.

"No you don't," the voice said. The rubbing on his chest became more excited and exciting. He heard sobbing and choking and knew it wasn't him. The hands were moving down his body and a weight came on his chest. It was warm, so he didn't mind it. Nor did he mind that the hands were at his groin and doing very nice things. As a matter of fact the warm weight was all over his chest and abdomen. It moved around very excitedly. For some reason, his opening his eyes had made it very happy. He opened them again and groaned.

"That's it, Jason, come back to me. We have to get you out of this."

The weight shifted and moved toward his stomach and thighs. He tried harder to focus. Slowly, before him, the backside of a naked woman lying chest down on his stomach, legs spread before his face, took form. He knew he was dreaming now.

"Shit," the female voice said. "You're not going to like this."

He was just getting aroused by her hands in his groin, when a ripping, tearing pain shot through that area. He doubled up by reflex, pulling his legs up and kneeing the female in the face. The whole scene somehow upset the floor, because it tilted toward his head. He started sliding and groaning because of the fire burning in his loins.

"Come on, Jason, we gotta be moving," the female voice said again when he came back to the world of light and pain. His groin throbbed and was slippery. He opened his eyes to see a naked woman, with a shaved head he almost recognized, playing with his injured area.

Reflexively he tried to jerk away from her. "Ep R nds wa f m," didn't come out like he wanted, but she seemed to get the idea. He didn't move like he wanted either, his body was wooden and stiff.

She rubbed tears and blood off her face with the back of her hand, "Ha, I got you moving at least," she said with a nervous laugh. "Do you know who you are? Who I am? Where we are?"

"*What kind of question was that for a woman who had just tried to rip your dick off to ask*?" he thought to himself. "O! I ," he wasn't talking out loud very well. He started looking around and thinking. His eyes went wild as he tried to remember. By the gods of space, he hurt.

"Good! You sit right there and I'll be back." She pushed herself to her feet with some difficulty and limped away.

He had no answers for her questions, just pain. The pain in his head was almost unbearable as he looked down at himself. His chest, stomach, and groin were covered in blood and hastily make bandages. He felt his head. It was hairless and he felt a pattern of welts and bumps on his scalp. He wanted desperately to be better. He wanted to remember. He wanted help. Tears of pain and frustration leaked out of his eyes.

Motion attracted his eye and he looked up to see a floating cylinder with arms. It was feeling good at him. Puzzled, he watched it float closer. When it was several centimeters away, it shot him with a blue green cloud and the world went dark again.

# XXVII

The warm hands were back and the female curves. He opened his eyes to see his partner, Falon, bending over him and pushing on his chest. She was naked and shaved bald. It all came back to him in a flash. "Don't touch me," he lurched under her hands and tried to back away.

"What?" Falon jerked away. She eyed him closely. "You talked."

"Damn right I talked! What are you trying to do to me? What happened to you?"

"Oh", Falon said, as her eyes welled up with tears and her hand went to her mouth.

Jason was shocked out of his anger by her reaction. He had never seen her cry before. Swear, spit blood, fiery eyed with anger, steely eyed for the kill, but never, ever cry.

She pulled her hand away from her mouth, "Who are you?"

Jason paused just an instant wondering if this was real, "I'm Jason McCullan and you're Falon, my partner. I'm the owner operator of the interstellar freighter Boundless and you're my junior partner." He remembered the last question she had asked, "I guess we are on the planetoid I discovered in the asteroid belt. It's obviously not as dead as we thought. I have no idea where IN IT we are or why you tried to rip my dick off."

She gave him a twisted smile, while angrily wiping the tears away. "You're right, we are on that damned to the sun planetoid you found in the asteroid belt near Delter. And I wasn't trying to rip your dick off, I was pulling the tubes out of your femoral arteries." She turned her head to reach for something and Jason noticed the two triangular metal looking plates mounted in her skull surrounded by red puffy angry skin. She turned back, handing him a set of cover-alls. "Can you get into these by yourself?"

"I don't know. I remember a lot of pain and you doing something to my .. ah .. ah .. body. Then this cylinder floated over to me." He shook his head, which didn't hurt any more, and added, "Is any of this making any sense to you?"

"Some of it. I don't know anything about the cylinder part, but you were in some kind of tube affair filled with fluid. You had a full head helmet on and tubes inserted into arteries at the neck, chest, and groin. You also had something attached to your abdomen. It looked like everything had stopped working, or wasn't working right, because you started turning blue. I pushed on the big red button and it dropped you on to that table." She pointed a narrow metal table covered with blood, tilted, and mounted inside a arched space. There were several manipulator arms hanging limp, partially extended inside.

Memories rushed into Jason. For some unknown reason, he was remembering what the device was and how it worked even though he had never seen one of them before. His head started hurting.

"What's wrong?" Falon asked.

"Why?"

Falon gave him the look she always did when he asked a stupid question, "Because your eyes went wild and started darting from side to side, like a pooka rabbit caught in a light."

"I started remembering what a Genetic Rehab was and how it worked, sort of."

"You remembered what?"

"That thing," Jason pointed at the device he had come out of, "is called a Genetic Rehabilitation and Repair Medic. Well sort of. I don't think the name translates right."

"Translates from what?"

Jason shook his head and ran a hand over his face. "I don't want to talk about it right now. This is all very confusing." He looked up at her and realized they were both very naked. He felt his face grow warm and other responses started. His partner was very attractive; one hundred and seventy seven centimeters tall, exceptionally well muscled, large breasts, proportional hips, and high cheek bones on a delicate face. "Why don't we get dressed." Jason didn't wait for a response. He virtually leaped up and slipped into his ill-fitting cover-alls. He was about one hundred and eighty eight centimeters tall and while not a muscle man, he wasn't a weakling either, but the cover-alls just hung off him.

"Why are you so spry? Thirty minutes ago I was pounding on your chest trying to get your heart beating," Falon asked in irritation.

Jason paused in consideration, "It must have been the floating cylinder thing. Yes, that was it. It provided me with a healing stimulant and growth field to bring about accelerated healing."

"Really," Falon started looking around, "Where did it go? I could use that real bad right now."

Jason felt terrible as he realized that if he was in the genetic rehab section of the facility, then Falon must have been here as well and he hadn't thought once of what had been done to her. "How do you feel?" he asked full of concern.

"I feel like shit. One of them damn machines put these plates in my skull." She paused to grit her teeth and start putting on her cover-alls. Jason tried not to watch. "I must've been in one of those things too, because I woke up over on that table." She pointed across the room to another table in an arch. She struggled to roll up sleeves and cuff the legs.

"You want me to help?"

"No! Yes! I want you to find that damned healing machine and get it back over here." Falon growled as she struggled to her feet to finish pulling on her clothes.

Jason didn't know what to say. He was getting some very strange feelings and he was sure they were not his. He didn't want to explore that right now. There were too many things that he didn't understand and didn't want to try to sort out right now. They needed to get out of whatever this place was, before it decided to do something else to them.

He started concentrating on the mobile medic and how to get it back. Once again a series of memories, not his, flashed through his mind followed by a strange sensation of reaching for something without moving his hands. Across the room a meter long, roundish cylinder rose into the air and drifted toward them.

"Did you do that? Is that the healing thing? Is it voice actuated?" Falon asked.

"Ah,... I don't want to talk about it right now."

The device floated over to Falon, an arm extending from an internal compartment, then a spray of bluish green gas washed into her. It seemed to instantly be absorbed. Jason caught her as she slumped and eased her to the floor. The device slowly moved up and down the length of her body humming slightly, then drifted back over to where it started.

Jason stared at it in fascination. Circuits, schematics, structures, materials, system diagrams, and manufacturing procedures flashed before his eyes as he tried to understand what it meant. His head started hurting, almost blinding him with the pain.

"What happened?" Falon asked.

"It healed you."

"It did? It did! I don't feel like I'd been hit by a loader sled anymore." She looked over at him. "So what's wrong with you now? Is this only temporary?"

"No, it's not temporary. My head started hurting as I thought about that healer." Jason looked up from his hands and knees, "We need to get out of here. I don't understand what's happened, but something definitely is wrong with me."

Falon gave him a wry smile, "Gosh, not me," she said in a coy feminine voice, "I've always had metal plates in my hairless head."

"You are feeling better. Do you know where the ship is?"

"Nope. This place is the extent of my knowledge."

"Gods, how I hate this," Jason sighed out loud and lay down. " I don't understand the process, but I'll try it again. Why don't you look around for anything we could use." He ignored Falon's response as he concentrated on the Boundless. Her structures and systems seemed to leap into his mind's eye. With them firmly in mind, he tried to question where she might be berthed. Slowly, as he tried several different ways to visualize the question, a sensation of general direction grew in him. Standing, he rotated a few times until he had a good feel for which way.

"What are you doing?"

"I'm trying to feel which way the ship is!"

"Say what?"

Jason rounded on her, embarrassed by his suggestion that he could feel his ship. "You got a better idea? This is all I've come up with. I don't understand what's happened, but I do know that I can feel things I couldn't before and memories that I didn't make are in my head."

Falon frowned, "This is weird, but I don't have any other ideas. Lead on."

Jason was getting more of the complex emotions, so instead of trying to puzzle it out, he had the healing machine heal him again. Then he started feeling his way toward the Boundless. He soundlessly called for the floating healing machine to follow them. It rose and floated after them like a faithful hound.

They made their way slowly down corridor after corridor, past massive and complex machinery and spaces. The motion seemed to help the healing process. They stumbled less as time went on. Each of them used the healing machine several times before it stopped working. A growing certainty came to Jason as they walked among the equipment. "This place is breaking down." Falon didn't comment. Jason turned to look at her. He had been concentrating so hard on feeling the way, he hadn't noticed she was wearing a backpack. "What did you find?"

"Portable Med kit, tool kit, a couple of hand weapons, a couple of blankets, and a backpack."

"Are you sure?"

Falon's face clouded over, "I think I know what a backpack is."

"Not that, the other stuff. It's not that I doubt you or anything. It's just this technology is beyond ours and I was wondering how you knew."

Falon paused for a moment frowning, "I read the labels on the storage cabinets. I'm experiencing some memories as well. Or maybe they're just deep teach techniques we are not familiar with. I was involved in some research with deep learning several years ago and this seems to remind me of it. I think this is the product of that Educator you wanted to find."

"I didn't know you were involved with research!"

"There's a lot you don't know about me."

"That's because you never talk about yourself." Falon did a sideways nod and gestured that they move on. As always, Jason let it drop.

They trudged for hours, rested twice, found water, walked some more, slept, found another floating healing machine, used it, slept, ate, walked, and walked more. They saw the same things: extensive machinery, huge mysterious devices, small mysterious devices, but never any people. Jason found that he shouldn't concentrate on anything for too long, otherwise he would start remembering what it was, how it worked, and get a severe headache. Falon's "memories" were more along the language and weapon lines. She would see something and remember what it was, and did, and how to shoot it or defend against it. They also found out that the lights would turn on just before they arrived at a section and turn off after they left. They figured the heat worked the same way, mainly, because they ran across several sections where one or the other or both didn't work. Falon had found a hand lamp earlier, so they had light.

They quickly lost track of time. They would walk until they were tired or sick, sleep, eat, use what healing devices they could find, walk more. It seemed like they had been here forever. They were just getting up from a rest and packaging their equipment when Falon noticed a light approaching. They pulled out the weapons and waited. A wheeled flatbed hauler rolled to a stop in front of them and Jason started feeling a complex series of emotions. They definitely were not his. He thought about it for a moment and they seemed to resolve into a form of communication, non-verbal communication. He concentrated on what it was instead of how and the message gradually got clearer.

"It's communicating with me." Jason finally told Falon.

"Okay, what's it saying?"

"Well, I think it's trying to tell me it will take us to the Boundless. I thinks it's complaining about how long we are taking."

"What the hell! I don't care. If it will give us a ride, I'll give it a go." Falon threw her pack on to the hauler, then crawled on. Jason shrugged and followed her.

As soon as they were settled, Jason thought "go" at it and they started moving. The hauler slowly built up speed until they were feeling a steady wind across their faces. It was moving at a very good clip. They passed through hundreds of different areas, before it pulled into an immense cavern they recognized. In the center, dwarfed by several other structures, was the Boundless.

She rested on a pad easily twice her size, with cables and tubes running from her. All her access hatches were open with devices, large and small, coming out. Most of the devices appeared to have manipulator arms and other forms of work aparati. As they got closer, they watched the Tigerous lifted and pushed back into her launch bay. Across the hanger from the Boundless was an Imperial ship in a state of disassembling. Even as they watched more was being removed.

Jason was horrified by what they might have been doing to his ship. As his consternation increased, so did the speed of departure of the various devices. By the time they reached the ship, the access hatches had been closed and the cables taken away. Jason was furious. This place had violated his ship.

"Are they done? "

"What?" Jason growled.

"What's your problem?"

Jason rounded on her, "My problem?" he virtually shouted. "My problem is that these machines have been messing with my ship. I didn't ask them to. They had no right."

Falon looked at him for a moment, then burst out laughing. The madder he got, the louder she laughed. Finally, Jason reached over and pushed her off the loader. Luckily, it wasn't moving very fast by then. So, Falon only rolled a little bit, then lay on the floor laughing. Jason was appalled by what he had done. He realized that he had meant to hurt her and that he no longer had strange "feelings" about things. By the time Falon had stopped laughing and was walking toward him, he had himself under control again.

"So, why were you laughing at me?"

"It's nothing. Forget it."

"No. I want to know."

Falon sighed loudly and shouldered her backpack. "Let's get on the ship." She turned away and walked toward the Boundless.

Jason crossed his arms and didn't move. "No. I want to know why you laughed at me. We are going to sit right here until you tell me."

"Suit yourself," Falon walked to the lower hatchway. It wouldn't respond to her palm press. She opened the small access panel and tried the key sequence, nothing. "Jason, the hatch won't open."

"So. We aren't going anywhere until you tell me why you were laughing."

Falon tiredly let the backpack slide off her shoulder to rest on the ramp way as she leaned her head against the ship. She leaned there for several minutes then turned around and sat down with her back to the door. Looking at Jason, she waved for him to come over and patted the ramp next to her. Jason slowly walked over to her and sat down. "It's like this," she began. "We have been raped and violated in the worst possible way. You're a guy, so being raped never crosses your mind, it's different for women. It seems to be the first thing done to us. Anyway, our bodies have been penetrated with devices, our minds have been altered, and the gods only know what has been done to us." She absently rubbed the metal triangle in her head through the stubble of hair. "You almost die in one of those machines, tubes had been inserted into ... I don't want to think about that. And after all that and probably more we don't even know about yet, the point when you get mad enough to kill something comes when you realize that your ship has been worked on without your consent." She smiled at him then looked away, "It was just so you, that I lost it." She turned back to him with a strange look in her eyes, "You are so weird, so special. You never cease to amaze me."

That was the longest speech Jason had ever heard Falon make. Somewhere in the middle of it he had stopped being mad. He realized the strange mixed up feelings were back and very strong. He flushed, felt cold and tingly, and hot at the same time. "Ah mmmmm...Perhaps we should get the ship out of here now?" Jason reached around behind him and pulled on a small lever, then stood and pulled another lever in the access panel. The door clicked and started to rise. Falon shook her head and stood up. With one hand, she effortlessly lifted the door the rest of the way.

"So, why didn't the door open for me when I put in the code?"

"They would've shut all the power off in the ship, even disconnected the batteries, if they were going to make extensive repairs. You hit the unlock sequence, I manually initiated it." Jason studied the door track and other surfaces before he stood up with a puzzled look. "Falon, do you know how much that door weighs?"

"No. It didn't feel like much."

"Really, never mind." Jason shook his head slightly, turned and ran his head into the upper combing of the hatch as he tried to step through. Falon did the same thing.

"Shit," She exclaimed, "they lowered the hatchway. Why in all the hells would they do that?"

Jason looked around alarmed. The passageway looked different to him. "Come on, but stay low. Something isn't right here. We should stay together until Fred is online."

Jason led the way to the aft engineering section main power control terminals. Everything seemed smaller than he remembered. He hit his head several more times before he learned to bend lower. The main battery breakers had been opened, killing all power to the ship. With an expert hand, Jason deftly closed and sealed them. Lights and ship noises started up all over. Jason stepped over to a panel and pressed several other switches. Then aloud he said, "Fred!"

At first nothing happened, then the speakers blared, "Intruders in engineering! Stand fast and nothing will happen to you."

"Fred, this is Jason and Falon, initiate voice recognition sequence and retype."

"Very clever, whoever you are, but voice pattern is only sixty-four percent."

"What the shit? Jason how do we...." Falon started to say.

Jason cut her off, "Override initiate, epsilon alpha three nine hexteen fox-trot charley fox-trot initiate initiate initiate, start now Fred, over and out."

"Copy override, you have twelve seconds to prove identity."

Jason motioned for Falon to remain quiet, "First equation, helicity."

"Standing by."

Jason recited the ion lens equation which was based on the principle of magnetic fields joining exactly perpendicular to each other and the binding elements of the gravaton field perpendicular to the junction of both. "Wrong, bilge rat," Fred announced with venom.

"Second equation, hyperspiral graviton encompassing field," Jason didn't wait for Fred to say anything, as he started to recite the equation for the graviton field which surrounds a ship in interstellar flight, partially nullifying the mass of a vessel and enabling hyperspace travel.

"Wrong again, standby to suck vacuum. Last try?"

"Fred there is no last try. Two plus two equals four."

"Welcome aboard, Jason. Where did all this new equipment come from? What are the modifications to my weapon system, and when did I get a weapon system? I tried to resist Jason, but the planetoid was too strong. It drained all my energy and over-road the backups."

"Initiate new voice print and recognition sequence. Start full ship diagnostics. Falon and I will be in the galley. Don't worry about losing the fight, Fred. Right now, I just want off this rock!"

"Nice to have you back, Falon."

"Thanks Fred, why didn't you recognize our voices?"

"They are different. I recommend you both report to medical for complete physicals before we lift ship."

"That's a good idea Fred, Jason and I will do that right now."

"What, we have a great deal of work to do before we lift ship, why would we need to go to medical?"

"Well," Falon began while giving him the don't ask stupid questions look and rubbing one finger over a metal plate, "Let's see, we both spent an unknown time immersed in bioengineering equipment which was making some kind of alterations to us. We haven't eaten right for days. We both seem to be taller than we were before and our voices have altered. It's been awhile since I went through a change of life like this and I wasn't expecting to do it again for a number of years."

Jason smiled, "Open mouth, talk, then engage brain."

Jason spent a few minutes turning on power and securing panels in engineering then he and Falon started forward. A general feeling of uneasiness began to creep over him as he marched along counting junction boxes showing signs of having been opened and new odd colored boxes mounted near cable bundles. When they started through the galley, Jason turned and stopped at a drink dispenser.

"What are you doing? You don't need a drink. I thought we were going to medical?"

"I don't want to right now." Jason stopped as his coffee arrived. "I ah....I don't want to know what's happened to me yet."

Frowning, Falon leaned up against one of the partitions, "Why?"

Jason stared into his coffee and frowned, "I'm not sure, but I think we should get out of here first, then try to reconstruct what happened."

"Why?"

"I have this bad feeling that this place isn't done with us yet and I don't want to give it any more time."

Falon sighed, "I use to be the one to get feelings. Aren't you the one with the sign that reads 'In God I Trust, All Others Bring Data.' Where's your data?"

Jason took a long pull from his coffee, "Okay, here's how I read this. This rock is dying after all these years. It needs something it doesn't have and the resources aren't close by, otherwise it could send one of it's machines to harvest whatever was needed and bring it back. That's where we come in. Why did it do to us what it did? Why did it let us get back to the ship? Why was the ship modified with add on tech instead of rebuilt?" Falon scowled while in thought. "Why would it take an obviously inferior technology vessel and crew and modify them to a new specification using precious dwindling resources?"

"By hell! We're to be its slaves!"

"Exactly. I don't know why its waited but it has. Perhaps it has run out of energy, or lost track of us, or is waiting for us to heal up. I don't know, but I don't want to wait. Fred, can you do a biomass scan on us at this location?"

"Let's get the hell out of here!" Falon stated.

"I can't get a good reading because of other interference."

"Can you tell if we have any active devices in our bodies?"

"My internal electromagnetic interference sensors detect no emissions from either of you."

"Fred, initiate emergency start sequence of fusion fuel torroids. Put all backups on line. Initiate primary engine cycling using battery power."

"Jason, this is all against procedure. After extensive overhaul or an extended down period, procedures call for extensive diagnostics and shake down."

"What, you haven't finished diagnostics yet?" Jason winked at Falon. "Fred, this is a deep space emergency and it calls for drastic measures."

"Aye, aye sir. Emergency start sequence of fusion fuel torroid started, twenty minutes to emergency temperature and pressure for feed. All backups on line, there are several anomalies in the power lines. I can't account for the fluctuations, request human compensation. Primary engines cycling on battery power, battery power indicates five thousand percent of rated capacity, request human compensation. Torroid fuel insertion started, feed indicates forty percent increase in line levels, request human compensation. Torroid vacuum established, two hundred percent efficiency increase, request human compensation. Jason your presence is requested on the bridge. All systems are operating outside of known parameters."

"On my way Fred, light off the engineering console and feed all anomalous data to it. Stop engine cycling and fuel cell power up." Jason bolted for the door as he was talking. "Falon this will probably take awhile."

Falon smiled after Jason, shaking her head while she walked to medical. "Fred, power up the med unit and have it stand by for a complete physical exam." She stripped her overalls off and climbed into one of the receptacles. "At least one of us will be sensible about this."

"Med unit is on line and standing by. I agree, Jason should be checked out as well."

"Proceed." A series of beeps sounded and a sweep arm passed over Falon's body from foot to head then back to foot. A needle was inserted into her arm and blood drawn off. Falon fell asleep lying in the warm receptacle.

# XXVIII

"Falon to the Bridge!" Jason's voice startled her out of a nap. The Med unit was idle, an indication that it had finished her exam. She hopped out feeling pretty good, and began to dress.

"Good morning Falon, would you like the results of your exam?"

Falon proceeded to the bridge at a fast walk, "No Fred, store all the data and bring up the pilot console and weapons panel."

"Aye, aye sir."

Jason sat in front of his engineering console with hands in constant motion as Falon entered the Bridge. She noted several panel changes and her pilot chair had a different headrest. The holonav was different as well. "Fred, do you have the technical readouts for the equipment changes on the bridge?"

"Yes, I do."

"Please bring them up on the aux engineering station."

"Station powered up and waiting for use."

"Did you have a nice rest?" Jason asked.

"Yes, it wasn't my intention to take a nap, but it felt nice. You look like shit."

"That's okay. It matches how I feel. You slept about twelve hours."

"What! Why didn't you wake me?"

"I did, " Falon could feel Jason's smile without having to look at him, "when I needed you. It took longer than I thought to get the Boundless ready for lift off. They added all sorts of stuff. I spent the last several hours trying to figure out what it does, whether it will affect our departure, and how to shut some of it off. I don't know what it all does and I hope it won't matter, ha. Study the system data I compiled and see if it makes sense. The engines are warming. We can lift when you're comfortable. You've got to fly her, I just fix her."

Falon smiled despite herself. Jason had been saying that for years. She turned her attention to the engineering station and the new system information. It was fascinating and confusing. The ship's power speed ratios were way beyond anything she had ever piloted. The little interstellar freighter had more thrusting power than warships a thousand times her volume. Sensors, navigation, computation, weapons were off the scale as well. She couldn't take it all in. Rubbing her eyes she laid her head against the modified headrest on the chair.

"TCI initiated," Fred announced. Bright colors and smells flashed through Falon's mind. "Calibration and optimization sequence start." Flashes of pictures and feelings streamed across the station monitors. She wanted them to slow down so that she could study each of them individually and they did. It was as if she was holding the ship and turning it with her hands, feeling the performance changes and system capabilities. Data flooded by her at an incredible rate. She remembered it all.

"*Feel changes*," she thought suddenly, "*You can't feel changes on a monitor*." She shot up out of her chair, a snapping pain in her head left her panting and shaking.

"TCI initiating remote mode," Fred chimed. Images exploded into Falon's minds' eye again.

"Stop TCI," Jason's voice boomed. Falon slumped to the floor. "Fred, definition of TCI."

Jason rushed over to help her up. "Get away from me," she raged, throwing him across the bridge into a panel. She turned and smashed her hand into the aux engineering station, denting the metal front plate.

"Thought Communication Interface, TCI, bioengineering method of telepathy. The system is to allow thought interface with all ship's navigation...."

"*Greeting slaves*," a voice boomed out on the bridge. Falon turned to see a disembodied head floating over the modified holonav unit while Jason picked himself up off the deck. "I sense this ship is operational, so it is time for you to begin your mission."

"You can go to all the hells of space you..." Falon raged

"TCI remote mode initiating," Fred chimed. Falon stopped in mid rant eyes wild as she froze in position.

The head turned towards her, "*Servants can either be punished*, "Falon screamed as her body swayed and twitched, "*or rewarded*," she took a deep breath and moaned longingly. Tears were streaming down her face as she continued to pant and moan. It was more debilitating than the pain. She slumped to the floor once more trembling, twitching, panting, moaning, and crying.

Jason watched in horror as Falon was tortured so casually. Speculation about thought interfacing had gone on for centuries and he was getting to see the worst of it. The Empire had several research projects on it when Jason was on active duty and had even fielded a physical connection version, which required a plug to be installed in the subject's head. Fighter pilots were the recipients.

"*Pilot take your station*," the head ordered. Falon started pulling herself towards the pilot chair unable to stop. The head turned to Jason, "*MynLord your mission is to collect several tons of rare minerals and return as soon as possible. Your ship's archaic computer has been supplied with the necessary information.* "

"I don't think so," Jason replied with barely controlled rage. "Who are you and what is the meaning of this?"

The head frowned, pressure started in Jason's head but, while uncomfortable, it didn't hurt. "*I am the Guardian, you and your warrior pilot have been conscripted into service of the Duoian cause. You will act as our agent for acquiring the materials we need from the barbarian cultures around us.*"

"I think not! We barbarians call this piracy and I won't be a party to it."

"*You are more intelligent than your warrior pilot, so I didn't think it would be necessary to demonstrate the pain, pleasure process, but it seems I was mistaken.*" The pressure increased on Jason's head but still didn't hurt.

"Fred, voice override all communication functions and shut down power to the boxes indicated in zap503."

"Override initiated and successful. Power shut down being blocked."

Jason leaped over the holonav, passing through the head, and slid to a stop in front of the bridge power panel. He quickly pulled several breakers and interlocks.

"Power shut down completed."

Falon sighed, "Thank you."

"Lets get engines powered up and find out how to get out of here." Jason steadied himself on the back of a chair.

"*VarLord forgive me.*" The head was still over the holonav and looked shocked. "*I mistook you for a lesser creature. It is obvious that your mental powers are greater than anticipated. Our need is great, the minerals are vital to our continuation. I debase myself before you, we are your servants in this need.*" The head bowed in supplication.

"Fred, why is power still being applied to the holonav?"

"It isn't Jason."

"The head is still hovering over it."

"What head Jason? I detect no plasma emissions."

"Serve me then by opening the space port doors," Jason demanded of the head, "and provide my pilot with a course out of here."

"*Your pilot is no longer interfaced. Manual coordinates are available through the archaic computer. The port will be opened as you command. VarLord, I implore you to make haste. Our continued survival depends on your success. I beg of you not to hold my miscalculation of your rank and prowess against us.*"

"Making haste is exactly what I had in mind." The pressure on Jason's head was getting worse and starting to hurt. He used both hands to steady himself.

"I have the coordinates Jason. I will feed them to the navigation panel," Fred's smooth tone offset the tension.

"I have coordinates on the grid and locked into flight path. Standing by to lift on your say Jason." Falon's hands were rock steady even if the rest of her was trembling. The four forward visual panels began to show the inside of the hangar bay. The aft display was showing a large section of the wall moving, opening to provide a way out.

"Initiate lift off," Jason commanded as he moved unsteadily over to his engineering console.

Falon didn't hesitate. A gentle buzz sounded throughout the ship as the graviton fields were established. The monitors indicated upward movement and horizontal axial rotation. Positioning thrusters fired briefly, propelling the Boundless toward the door. Once Falon had her lined up, she hit the main thrusters hard shooting them through the opening. With open sky above, she rotated them onto the aft engines and blasted with quarter power to the ion engines. The Boundless leaped away from the planetoid.

"Shields up!" Jason screamed! "Deflectors at full power! Falon, what the hell are you doing?!? Slow this thing down before we hit an asteroid."

"Shields are energized, deflectors are at full power and on automatic targeting. All systems are functioning normally. I think," Fred reported.

"I'm getting the hell off this rock. I won't hit anything." She concentrated for a moment while dodging a rock. "She handles like a fighter." There was awe in her voice, "Look at that acceleration."

"Well she isn't one, so drive a freighter." Jason watched as Falon slowed them down and started plotting a saner course. "But I think they turned the tug into one," Jason added with a smirk.

Falon looked over at him, "One what?"

Jason smiled, "A fighter." Falon had wanted to buy one for the ship since becoming a full partner, but they could never afford it.

"A weapon has fired. One moderate delta V rock has been vaporized," Fred reported matter of factly.

Falon's attention jerked back to the screens. "What weapon?"

"I don't know what it was. It fired from the port bow by modulating a complex energy stream through the hyperspace field antenna. I think."

"Fred," Falon sighed, "this 'I think' stuff is getting old. You either know or you don't know."

"Untrue. My systems have undergone extensive modification just as yours have. Also, like your systems, I am continuing to change even now."

Jason frowned, "Continuing modifications, are there builder programs running within your systems?"

"What do you mean by, 'continuing to change like my systems?'" Falon said at the same time. "What kind of changes?"

"A weapon has fired, the deflectors. One high delta V rock has been vaporized. It was definitely achieved by modulating a complex energy stream through the hyperspace field antenna, starboard quarter." Fred reported.

"Falon, slow down!" Jason ordered.

"Aye, aye sir," Falon responded as her hands move with machine like precision across the controls.

Jason took a deep breath, "Let's take this one step at a time. First, let's get out of this asteroid belt, then we will analyze the data relative to our system modifications. Okay?" Falon nodded, yes. Jason turned back to his console, "I'll start with Fred and see if I can narrow down what's been done to him."

"I would rather you started with us. I'm rather upset by the thought that changes are continuing to happen to my body and I don't know what they are."

Jason was quiet, "Jason?" Falon asked.

He sighed deeply, "I'm not...I don't...I ah, I want to do that together."

"Jason, consider your body another ship and you need to start damage control on it. I will pilot us out of the asteroid field and you can talk to me about what you are discovering. At the speed we are moving now, this isn't a challenge. The Boundless handles like a dream, so I can divide my attention."

"Okay. Okay. I'll start the analysis on Fred and then go to sick bay for a diagnostic scan." After a few moments of hasty input Jason got up and left the Bridge.

Falon waited for a few moments, "Fred, where is Jason at now?"

"His lab."

"Shit. He's not going to come out of there until he's done with you is he?"

"He is proceeding to process the data necessary to understand system modifications to the Boundless as well as you and himself. His behavior is most irregular."

Falon started laughing while crying.

# XXIX

Jason glanced over the technical data provided by Fred's diagnostic programs, on the ship and on Falon. Then he sat and thought hard about the ship systems and the changes to them. He rode out the headache, the shakes, and hot flashes, while trying to understand the system changes. Finally, he couldn't stand the pain anymore, reported to the med unit, ordered a full diagnostic scan, and pain killers. He fell asleep digesting the details of the Boundless's new weapon system.

He woke to see a huge hairy, fanged, bipedal creature with clawed hands sitting across from him. Jason leaped to his feet and started backing away.

"Physical motion isn't necessary," a rich baritone voice announced. "I'm in your head, so you won't be able to back away."

Jason stopped moving, "You're that creature I was hauling from Delter?"

"In life I was. In life I gave you the gift of change which seems to have been accelerated. Now, I'm a teaching algorithm from your subconscious mind. It's time for a lesson. Your abilities have been augmented by a recent change."

"What? What abilities?"

"Those inherited from your parents, released by my gift of change, and augmented by recent events. Sit down and relax. The time is now and the lesson shall begin."

Jason felt a swirling sensation in his head accompanied by sensations and a decreasing pressure. "I'm not going to remember any of this am I?"

"You will retain the essence of the lesson, yet not remember the source."

"Great."

# XXX

"Jason, it's time to wake up." A soft voice said, accompanied by a gentle shake of his foot.

"What?" Jason bolted up right eyes darting wildly around. "Oh. Right, I must've fallen asleep. I had the strangest dreams. It all started with that asteroid...." His eyes fell on Falon, now blue eyed with a three inch growth of silver white hair. She was taller than he remembered, with very muscular arms and legs, well-proportioned shoulders, chest, waist and hips. She looked like one of the main players right out of his wildest sex fantasies.

Falon sat still letting him stare at her, his mouth hanging open in shock.

"Not a dream." Jason finally said.

Falon nodded, "Not a dream. At least not that part. What other dreams did you have?" she smiled suggestively.

"Quite a number. I seemed to have been visited by that creature from the Delter trip and the talking head from the planetoid. It's all blurring together now."

"How do you feel? Any headaches?"

Jason turned his head slowly from side to side, "No headaches, I feel pretty good."

Falon let out a sigh, "Good. I was pretty worried about you. Your brain hemorrhaged or at least that's what the med unit diagnosed. We don't think it got it quite right. Fred was hard pressed to come up with a treatment. You seem to be resistant to a large number of medications now, just as I am."

Jason squinted and frowned, "How long?"

Falon shrugged and slid out of her chair, "Fifteen days."

Watching her move distracted Jason. He was almost overwhelmed with a barrage of complex emotions, then it was like a filter sliding into place. The emotions resolved themselves into identifiable items. He knew that Falon was very worried and relieved at the same time. She had very strong "feelings" about his personal well being, among other things he wouldn't allow himself to explore. "Fifteen days! Where are we now?"

"We're at the edge of the asteroid field anchored to a big rock. I didn't want to take us out until you were awake and feeling better. I don't like the feel of things. So I though we could spend a few days working through what's happened to us and the ship."

Jason hopped down from the receptacle and almost collapsed to the floor. Falon moved with unbelievable speed to catch and pick him up. She held him easily in a standing position. "You've been real sick," Falon whispered. It was accompanied by another wave of emotion. "Let me help you to the mess deck. You're probably hungry."

"How strong are you?"

Falon shrugged, "Real strong. I've been eating many, many times my normal calorie intake, mainly in protein and mineral supplements. I've gained about a hundred pounds, none of it fat, and ten centimeters in height. I've spent my time in the med unit as well." Falon shook her head, "The medical programming we have isn't able to handle what's happening to us. Fred has reported similar changes in you as well. We need to find a really good doctor. This isn't over yet," she finished up as she sat Jason in a chair on the mess deck. When he saw the food laid out he couldn't contain himself.

"Well that answers the question about whether you're hungry or not."

Jason was eating too much to talk. He really wanted a console so that he could continue the investigation into ship alterations.

"*TCI initiated*," he heard Fred say. Then data started appearing to him. He sputtered food all over as he choked.

"Jason, what's wrong?" Alarm sounded in Falon's voice.

"Didn't you hear Fred, the TCI initiated."

Falon looked puzzled for a moment, then pursed her lips, "It only works for me on the Bridge. You must have a wider range. Fred said that the interface boxes were located throughout the ship. It must be for you." She leaned over and grabbed his hand, "Jason, you're a telepath."

"What!" Telepaths were hated and feared throughout the Empire. They were very rare. There had been at least one rebellion started by telepaths, and several others blamed on them. Being known as a telepath was not conducive to good health.

"Fred and I puzzled it out while you were asleep."

Jason thought about it while he finished eating. "Okay, I guess I knew that. I was denying it, but I knew. The way I feel things now. All the stuff that happened on the planetoid." He filled his plate with another large helping of food. "What else have you pieced together?"

Falon got herself a cup of coffee, some tidbits to snack on and delivered her brief in a no nonsense tone. "You left the Tigerous in your assualt armor to explore the planetoid. We had set up Cryton as a retransmission station while you explored around the station. You found a workshop right next to the hangar and opened a door. We lost coms with Cryton about then. The door shut and you started trying to blast a way out. I pulled in close to use the plasma arcs to cut the door down, but by the time I got through you were being hauled away. I blasted my way out and returned to the Boundless. A couple of days later the Boundless was pulled to the planetoid and I was extracted from the ship. We woke up at about the same time, eighty-nine or so days later, and made our way back to the ship. I'm guessing it took us two maybe three weeks of walking and a day on the sled. Do you remember the rest?"

"Yeah. We blasted off and I went into the med unit." Falon smiled. Jason was struck anew by her beauty, full lips, blue eyes, sculptured cheekbones, and long eyelashes. She was also sending him a full set of sensual emotions.

A single tear appeared in her eye and started down her cheek. He was overwhelmed with the desire to comfort her. Jason reached over the table to gently stroke the back of her hand. He wanted desperately for her to need him, so that he could take her into his arms and comfort her. She slid her chair around so that he could put his arms around her. She rested her head on his shoulder and cried. Jason cooed softly, while, stoking her back and telling her it was all right now. Emotions were raging now, washing against him and getting sent back to her. Passion flared and different instincts took over. Jason wasn't in very good physical shape, so Falon was very careful not to over tax him.

Jason woke up ravenously hungry in Falon's arms. He felt embarrassed and relieved at the same time, but he didn't understand why. He carefully extracted himself without waking her and made his way to the mess deck. Lots of food and thought was in order.

"*It's called an emotional feedback loop*," a familiar voice supplied. Jason dropped his fork as the hairy creature from the Plet trip walked on to the mess deck. "*One of the dangers of being an untrained telepath and confined in a small space, is the amplification of emotions feeding back and forth between two individuals. Strong emotions are the worst. You were lucky in this case.*"

"*Who are you?*"

The creature smiled at least Jason thought it was a smile, "*I'm dead, remember? This is your second lesson in filtering. Now pay attention.*" The creature showed Jason several ways to block emotions or channel back their effect on him. It also directed him toward several pieces of literature about self-discipline, meditations, and mind over body techniques, which would be directly applicable to a telepath. The creature left him with a compelling imperative to gain mastery of this before being confronted by a large population. Jason woke with a start, finished the snack, and went to find a terminal.

Jason studied, ate, exercised, and tried to stay away from Falon for the next several days as he struggled to get better physically and mentally. When they were together, he tried to filter the emotional exchange between them and maintain a rigid discipline. Falon spent most of her time on the bridge playing games through the TCI and getting more familiar with the ship's systems. Jason found his control of ship's systems through the thought interface getting better and better. He could absorb and process data at an incredible rate.

"We need to talk," Falon announced.

Jason went rigid exercising his fledgling mind control. "About what?"

"About what we are going to do next. What's your problem?" Falon frowned studying Jason, "Your concerned about us making love aren't you?"

"Ah, Well, yes." He wouldn't meet her eyes.

Falon studied him, "Why?"

"What do you mean why?"

"Why are you concerned?" She smiled slightly, "It is a rather natureal response to an extreme life threatening circumstances. We have been in each other's presence almost exclusive for the last several years. You are very attractive, now that the Civilization conditioning has been removed."

Jason was shocked, "You mean you liked it."

Now it was Falon's turn to be shocked, "You didn't?"

"No," Falon's gaze turned lethal, "No, I mean, yes. Yes, I did. It's just that I've never thought of you that way before. You've always been,...been,...well been my partner. A lady."

"So?"

Jason was moving his hands trying to articulate what he was feeling while maintaining rigid control of his emotions, but he wasn't saying anything.

"Jason are you concerned that your telepathy some how caused a primordial encounter?" Fred's interjection surprised them both.

"How did you come up with that?" Jason asked.

"You have been reading every article and manual on mental control, discipline, and telepathy in my memory banks. The psychiatry program provides several indicators as to sexual behavior between humans of the opposite sex and problems there of. And I've been receiving thought inputs from you having indications along those lines."

"You're reading my mind!"

"No, more like you're telegraphing your mind. However, the preliminary prognosis is that you two should talk about those circumstance so that you two can work it out and thus begin to live in harmonious sexual rapture."

Falon got up smiling, "I'll be on the Bridge. I refuse to receive advice on my sex life from a program."

"Fred's right," Jason blurted out before Falon could leave the room. Falon stopped and slow turned around. "I think I initiated a emotional feedback loop between us. Receiving spontaneous sensitive feelings from you then amplifying them and sending them back. Which you received and amplified, and so on until we couldn't help but jump each other."

"So?"

"So, it wasn't the spontaneous primal response that you think it was."

"Did you enjoy it?"

"What!" Jason fell deep into Falon's eyes, "Yes, it was the best sex I have ever had." He was confused by Falon's non-reaction. She had always been sexually distant and seemed put off by the idea from any male. He'd watched her deck quite a number of guys trying to score and not taking no for an answer.

Falon gave him a heart-stopping smile, struck a pose with one hand on her hip which instantly gave him ideas, and peaked one eyebrow. "Then I can't wait until you're up to full speed again." She turned and walked off the mess deck in such a way as to make him understand her intentions. "See you on the Bridge. We still need to talk about what's next and when. Our food supply won't last forever."

Jason was amazed by Falon's reaction. After a few minutes of collecting his thoughts and getting his emotions in line, he followed her to the Bridge.

"We have about four months of food left at our current rate of consumption," Falon announced unceremoniously as Jason walked on to the Bridge.

"Fred, bring up the holonav and display this sector." The unit hummed to life and the faint odor of ozone filled the air as the plasma field ballooned out. Jason walked over to study the display. "There are lots of places close enough for replenishing our stores."

"How safe are we going to be putting down in those places?"

Jason looked up frowning, "I don't understand what you're getting at? Why wouldn't we be safe, other then the normal Imperial angles?"

Falon smiled, "Well, the Empire was after this ship before and now it has technology installed which the Empire would kill to get their hands on. They tried to kill you before. Think about what they would be willing to do now. You and I don't look the same, but all our identification is known. As soon as we set down and log in someone will be interested. You aren't Civilized anymore, the Imperial scum at Plet were suspicious, and we have removed the Imperial hound dog stuff from Fred. Not to mention, we still have the Shard's salvage on board."

"Shard's salvage is legal, but blast, you're right. It will raise questions I don't want to answer. I need to think about this. We need to get to a planet which isn't too rigid with regard to Imperial legalities, but safe enough for a small freighter like ourselves."

Falon snorted, "You've been a little too busy with your personal problems to really think about the tactical implications of this ship's capabilities." Jason gave her a questioning look. "Have a seat Jason and let me brief you on tactical." Falon walked to the main viewing screens. "Fred, bring up the tactical system data in my new game file."

The screens lit up with an image of the Boundless and Tigerous. "Let's start with the Boundless," She turned to point at the ship. "Max speed about point four of light, acceleration one hundred fifty times that of a freighter of this class, maneuverability forty-five times standard. This is without stressing the hull or mechanical systems. All achieved through electromagnetic and gravitonic field science advancements. This ship has the characteristics of a fleet frigate and a little more. Weapons, a single multiphase space/field warp energy cannon, I don't know what to call it. Except, it will fire a bolt every minute or so capable of bringing down shielding on anything up to a cruiser, according to the data you gave Fred. You'll have to refine the calculations on that. Fred and I were in over our heads. The new deflectors will double as a close in missile and torpedo protection system with a very high rate of fire. Once again you'll have to refine the calculation, but Fred and I put it at twenty to fifty inbound in a couple of seconds. Fleet doesn't have anything like it. They still rely on multi-barrel fusion cannon."

"Not really, they have a different weapon now that is more of a multi-barrel pulsed coherent beam weapon, or at least that was what they were getting ready to install on all new construction models six years ago."

"I still think this system is far superior."

"Agreed."

"So we are not an unarmed freighter. Then you add sensors. I don't pretend to understand how it's being done, but our range is several magnitudes greater then it use to be. Fred has been able to plot the exact location of each asteroid within five light minutes of us. Once again, way beyond what we should be able to do. There are other anti-scrambling measures it has as well, which will keep it from being jammed. So we have speed, acceleration, maneuverability, weapons, and sensors beyond what the best of the Imperial fleet has, I don't think we need worry about casual pirate interference."

"This is an impressive compilation of data, you don't mind if I double check some of your figures?"

"Absolutely not. As a matter of fact I would like you to as soon as possible, so that I can update my tactical models. I forgot to mention thought interface. It speeds the reaction to every event and reaction by thousands of times."

Jason frowned, "I remember. You aren't uncomfortable using it?"

"No." Falon didn't pause, "I wouldn't have done it given a choice, but it's installed now, so I'm going to make the best use of it."

"The Tigerous?"

"Ah yes, the Tigerous has had the same modifications. She's faster and more maneuverable than any fighter listed in the books and mounts a smaller version of the multiphase cannon and deflector system. Add the thought interface and we have something way beyond the Empire. They installed a true launch bay for her. So she can be in space within minutes of activation. She's great in combat, based on simulation."

"So, the conclusion is that we will not have to worry about anything in the freighter class. There are several bonded armed merchantman in the 200 kilo ton class, we should avoid and any warship larger then a frigate."

"That's a pretty large range," Jason admitted. "Valtair VII."

"What about it?"

"That's where I think we should go. It's not too far. Not too well controlled and it has extensive salvage and repair facilities. Several bonded carriers with mercenaries use it as a base, so the medical facilities should be up to what we need. And I know the owner of one of the salvage yards. He owes me a favor or two."

"I don't like Valtair."

"Why not?"

"There are some people there that would like to get their hands on me."

"That's where you and I joined up, wasn't it?"

"You don't remember?"

"Not exactly. I had been drinking and it seems things didn't clear up 'til just before we made planet fall on Stump."

"Drinking! You were positively polluted. You didn't stop drinking until we ran out of alcohol. Anyway, it worked out for me. I was being inconvenienced on Valtair, and you provided me a way out."

"Jason, your Civilized psychological profile indicates that alcoholism was a possible link to the Civilization process." Fred supplied.

"Come on Fred, I wasn't an alcoholic."

"Data would disagree with your statement."

A stilted silence followed Fred's statement, as Jason considered the information and Falon studied Jason. "Okay, Fred, I'll bite. Why?"

"Cross reference to the medical library indicates that alcohol releases certain inhibitions thus muting the guilt feeling associated with them. Possibly, being intoxicated would allow you to bypass several of the memory problems associated with being Civilized."

"Is this a theory Fred, or have you got solid data?"

"This is deductive reasoning along a logic path."

"We need to think about that aspect more, if you're sure Valtair is the right place," Falon interrupted.

"Why?"

"You think about it some more. Fred, you too. Compile data, then we will talk more."

"What is it you're not telling me?"

Falon turned on a devastating smile, "We'll talk." She turned back to the tactical briefing. "Fred, bring up the tactical overlay." An image appeared with several different colored ellipses centered on an image of the Boundless. "This is the tactical picture as we've been able to build it. The colors represent estimated weapons range, sensor range, and maneuvering envelope. Our primary battery has a range beyond any beamed energy weapon the Empire has fielded that I know of. As you can see, she's very capable." Falon turned back to Jason, "I've been running simulations and combat scenarios using these parameters. We can do a great deal more than anyone will ever expect."

Jason stood up, "Well, you two have been very busy. Let's plot a course out of the asteroids and on to Valtair. Then I'll start double checking your calculations." Falon nodded and they both moved over to the holonav together.

# XXXI

Jason had been in his shop for sometime as Falon maneuvered them out of the asteroids and steadied up on the course for Valtair. "Jason, could you come to the bridge?" Fred asked.

"On my way."

Falon was standing in front of the holonav when Jason walked onto the bridge. "We are being followed by asteroids," she stated without preamble.

"What?"

Falon pointed to three fuzzy circles on the holonav. They each had a course and speed displayed next to them. "Fred plotted these as asteroids when we were waiting for you to recover. Remember when we were describing the sensor's capabilities?" She waited for Jason to nod. "Well, this was one of the exercises we went through. Plot all the asteroids within a range. It turned out to be a very large range, but these three items were plotted. They started moving when we broke into free space. I don't know what to make of them."

"Fred?"

"They originally appeared as solid masses when I scanned the belt. Then they changed when we broke away from the debris and steadied out in clear space. They don't register as space craft, but they do have ion trails and some type of field distortions, at least I think that is what's being reported to me by the sensor modules."

Jason frowned as he looked at Falon. She shrugged. "Okay, put it on the engineering console and I'll take a look. Ya know," he started as he turned away, "This was a lot simpler when I understood all the systems."

Jason sat down and started evaluating the signals. As he thought about the sensors their capabilities became clearer. He seemed to be hovering in space looking at the fuzzies as they slowly resolved themselves into Imperial warships. A blazing headache brought him back to himself. "Shit, my head hurts," he announced. Something cold and metallic pressed against his neck, it hissed and he felt a pinprick at the same time.

"Whatever you were doing," Falon announced. "Stop it! Fred reported that your brain waves went off scale and possible damage was occurring. You need to go to medical again."

"We don't have time. Those fuzzy things are Imperial warships, a destroyer and two frigates."

"We have time. You haven't been out for long and I don't want you passing out. So shut up, get up, and start walking." Jason started to resist but Falon leaned closer, "I will carry you if I have too."

"You are a bully. Did you know that?" Jason said as Falon helped him to his feet. He shut up when he realized he needed help getting to his feet.

"Fred," Falon announced, "bring the med unit up to stand by."

"Med unit standing by. The fuzzies are closing."

"Increase speed to what our maximum use to be."

"Aye, aye Jason."

Jason allowed Falon to lift him into the med unit. The equipment came on smoothly and did its job. Jason felt tension ease from his head and the pain recede. "So what was that you gave me on the bridge and how did you know I would need it?"

Falon snorted, "You'd been sitting there without touching a key for three hours. I had Fred listen in on your unfiltered broadcast and figured it was going to hurt you."

"What? My head still hurts so you're going to have to explain slower."

"You were doing something telepathic and Fred explained that you were doing extensive modeling which was a strain. I figured it wouldn't be good for you. So I came down here and had the med unit prepare a dose of stuff for you. It's the same thing we were giving you before." The diagnosis arm swept over Jason, humming as it went.

Jason watched it for a moment then realized it had another function, which wasn't part of the original equipment. He thought a complex file name at Fred then said, "*Initiate.*" The telepathic part wasn't a good idea. His headache came back with a vengeance. Several drugs were injected into Jason, then the diagnosis arm moved back over him. It was humming a different tune the second time. Jason felt the pain and pressure in his head ease off, then abruptly stop.

"What did you do?"

"He accessed a new medical file. It provided the med unit with augmented diagnostic and healing capabilities." Fred paused for a moment then changed subjects.

"The fuzzies have increased speed drastically. If our data files are correct, they are all driving at near maximum thrust for warships of the classes you described."

"The med unit reports me cured, so let's go to the bridge. I just had an idea about how to resolve the fuzzies into contacts."

Just as they stepped on to the bridge Fred reported, "The warships just transmitted the Imperial shut down codes to us."

Jason looked at Falon, "Opinion?"

"We're damned if we do and damned if we don't. Let's run for it. If we kick it in the butt, we should make jump point about eight hours before they do."

"I agree. Let's run for it."

"Fred, initiate plan B," Falon announced.

"Aye, aye sir. Engines increased to ninety percent of maximum thrust. We are being hailed. One of the fuzzies is pulling ahead of the others. It must be the destroyer."

"Fred, modify our visual so that we look like we did before our visit to the planetoid, then put them on."

The main screens changed from a star pattern to show a blunt, pudgy faced Commander of the Imperial Navy. "Boundless, this is the Imperial Destroyer Poultinar, heave to." Jason knew the Commander as Walter Leegati, a friend from Jason's fleet days. Coincidence? Jason thought not.

"Why? We haven't done anything wrong." Jason noted that they had thirteen hours to jump point and that the Poultinar was going to be a scant five hours behind them.

"Because you have applied secret Imperial technology to your vessel which is against the registry laws, the civil laws, and your oath of retirement. By the sun, McCullan, we hold your ship at about point three five four of light and you have one tenth our mass."

"My ship hasn't had any secret Imperial technology applied to it. I made changes based on engineering journal releases and private discoveries. All very legal."

"If that's the case, then we will release you after we search your vessel."

"You plan on impounding my ship?"

"No, just searching it here in space. We aren't going to haul it off. If we don't find anything, you can go on your way." Walter frowned, "Ya, know Jason for someone that's been Civilized, you seem to have a lot of fight in you."

"Deep space emergencies seem to always come up." Jason smiled, "This has been the damnedest voyage. If it weren't for the alteration I made, we would be dead now."

"I can't wait to see what you've come up with this time." Walter's smile seemed genuine, "Heave to and let us board?"

"I'm sorry Walter, I don't believe you. Not you personally, just the fleet. If we stop, I think your orders are to make us disappear. Well, maybe not your orders, but PsySec I'm sure has their own plan." The captain of the Poultinar started to answer, then looked angry and shocked just before he glanced off to the side and the connection was broken.

"Walter?" Falon asked.

"He and I use to be friends. Walter Leegati was a shipmate of mine when we were ensigns. I went into the engineering side. He picked the command track. We followed each other's careers. He was at my promotion party when I made commander, four years ahead of him. I don't want to have to fight them. My guess is there is only one person on that ship that knows what's going on and it isn't her Captain."

"PsySec CO?" Falon asked.

Jason turned to look at her, "How did you know?"

"I had a run in with them several years ago, before I got my interstellar pilot's license. It almost kept me out of the business. They are not nice people."

"You don't know the half of it. If there is one part of the service that is rotten and corrupt that's it." Jason punched several keys and watched the analysis scroll by. "Fred, start bleeding some of the thrust energy into the jump coils. We are going to need to jump early."

"Already being done, Jason. After our last cruise, I made it part of the standard operating procedure and with the new efficiency level of the engines, it doesn't even detract from our speed. We will be at full jump charge in one hour fourteen minutes."

"Falon, if we jump..."

"I'm recalculating now."

Jason turned back to his own console and started running diagnostic data on the Poultinar and the Boundless. He used the data to update Falon's tactical profiles, updated Fred's sensor data structure, and calculate the probability of them escaping without having to fight.

"Okay, Jason are you ready?" Jason turned to look at her. "There is an easier way. Fred, initiate TCI. Think at it Jason. You need the practice, but don't think too hard and hurt yourself."

Jason smiled as he directed his awareness at the interface. The holonav seemed to blossom and fill his mind's eye. He saw the three dimensional image of the Boundless traveling through space as if he was above and behind her. This expanded out to show the closest star, then several more solar systems, and finally their destination.

"*This is the normal jump point, course, and terminus.*" Falon's voice filled his mind as colored dots appeared in relative position showing normal jump point, and planned course to terminus. "*If we jump early we have to jink over to compensate for this,*" a colored ring surrounded a solar system, "*star. It will add another jump, but take us off the routine path, which might throw off your friends. It has a safety margin of 95.*"

"*How much of this is assumption? You did this real fast.*"

"*None.*"

"*Fred, do you concur with the calculations?*"

"*Yes, Jason I do. Falon and I worked it out together. Error correction to sixteen decimal places, by the book.*"

"*How?*"

"*Thought interface,*" Falon replied. "*Like I told you before, communication and coordination is 1000 times faster.*"

"*Okay, let's do it. Make preparations to jump on the new coordinates.*"

"*Jason, we are being hailed by the Poultinar.*"

"*Okay Fred bring....No wait.*" Jason's visualized hands flashed across the board to access data. "*Okay Fred, edit the medical findings on my Civilization profile to remove any indications on how we found out. Just leave in the prognosis based on its continuation and stand by to transmit it on all wavelengths, not just communications channels.*"

"*Ready Jason.*"

"*Put them on.*"

The star field faded to show the Captain of Poultinar and a very handsome command rank individual. "Jason, this is Commander Lanker, the PsySec CO on Poultinar. He would like to assure you that there are no secret orders on how to handle you or your ship," Walter announced without preamble.

"Glad to meet you. I still don't believe you. I'll tell you what, you guys analyze the prognosis of what my being Civilized was doing to me, then we'll talk. It's really pleasant reading, you, Walter, should take special note since retirement is in your future. Until then, I'm cruising full speed ahead." Jason thought '*transmit*' at Fred.

"Jason, what's your game? We are receiving on all systems."

"Bridge communications can be censored. I want everyone on your ship and the other two to know what was done by PsySec to a highly decorated service veteran retiring after honorable service. Boundless out." Fred took the cue and cut the connection.

"Did it feel good?" Falon asked.

"Not yet. I don't expect anything to come of it either, but on the outside chance, I wanted to give them all something to think about. There is one thing every service member is sure of, if you're lucky, one, day you get to retire to the good life. I just shook that foundation."

Jason continued to refine the analysis of how the new systems would compare to existing Imperial technology and update the tactical picture. Falon recomputed the jump calculations and tested the updated tactical data against her models. The Boundless cruised ahead at speeds she was never designed to reach.

"Jason, we are being hailed again."

"Same as before Fred, then open a channel."

The Captain of the Poultinar looked upset, "Jason this is criminal. I don't know who did this to you, but I will find out."

Commander Lanker stepped into view, "You aren't Civilized anymore are you?" It wasn't an accusation. "Not that I would blame you."

Jason smiled, "No, but the Empire would. I didn't say the Civilization effects had been removed. Perhaps you understand my reluctance to heave to. I don't know what to expect anymore."

"Jason, I'm willing to escort you to the closest port to get this all sorted out. Something smells here and I don't want to be a party to it." The PsySec CO gave Walter a startled look. "It will be bending my orders, but that's why COs are given command flexibility." The Captain of the Poultinar was glaring at the PsySec Officer as he said the last.

"*Hyperspace terminus detected ahead.*" Fred announced. "*Ship has entered normal space. It is another fuzzy.*"

"What gives Walter? Another warship has jumped in ahead of us."

"What," the Poultinar's CO looked startled. He glanced over to something out of Jason's view. "How could you..."

"You're a telepath," Commander Lanker accused.

Jason realized he had received Fred's report via the TCI and that the new ship should have been out of their sensor range. "What?" He said, then severed the connection.

"How long to jump?"

"About ten minutes. How could he have known you were a telepath?" Falon asked.

"He was guessing? I don't know. I did just give away that our sensors were very long range though."

"Jason, the new fuzzy is on an intercept course. Time to intercept two hours four minutes. We are being hailed."

"Ignore it."

"Jason, I think the Poultinar just powered up her shields and kicked up her speed again," Falon announced. "She must be way over spec or they have something new."

"Probably the latter. How far behind us are they?"

"About four hours, maybe a little more."

They waited in tense silence as the minutes ticked by. "Jump point in one minute," Fred finally announced.

"Okay, start the count down. Stand by to jump," Falon took over smoothly. "Initiate TCI."

"*TCI initiated,*" Fred answered. She became the ship, looking over every jump system and power setting. "*Bring deflectors and weapon systems on line. Power up the hull shields.*" She ordered through the connection, all standard procedures.

"*All systems report ready,*" Jason answered through the telepathic link.

"*Now,*" Fred announced.

At the speed of thought, Falon released the stored energies tearing a hole in the fabric of space and throwing the ship into it. The Boundless winked out of existence in real space and shot into a tunnel drilled through hyperspace. A trip through hyperspace was normally several seconds of disorientation and queasiness followed by several hours of boredom. Plugged into the ship's sensors through the thought interface, turned it into an emotional experience. Vistas of electromagnetic confusion turned into indescribable visual imagery and abstraction. Interaction of the hyperspace fields with that area of space itself, created energy fields with fascinating complexities. It was over all too soon. Both Falon and Jason were left sitting wide eyed and panting in their chairs as the Boundless shot back into real space through the h-space terminus.

"*All systems normal and realigning navigational references,*" Fred announced.

Jason shook himself and looked around in wonder, "*Whoa, what a trip. Visualizing field interaction...*"

"*That was incredible. It was so beautiful,*" Falon added.

They both sat in a daze while the ship realigned itself, recalibrated it's systems, adjusted to the preset course, and sailed on at .4 the speed of light. Fred took care of everything.

"*Hyperspace Terminus detected aft,*" Fred announced. "*A warship has entered real space. There is an eighty seven percent probability it is the Imperial ship Poultinar. You both should report to the med unit for a complete diagnostic.*"

Both Jason and Falon looked around stupidly. "*What did you just report, Fred?*" Jason finally asked.

"*A warship has just jumped in aft of us. There is a ninety two percent chance it is the Poultinar. Both of you have sat unmoving for three hours and twenty eight minutes. Your biological minds were creating abstractions from the electromagnetic field distortions produced by our external sensors.*"

"*What are you talking about, Fred, we just went into h-space?*" Jason was still not thinking well.

"*Jason, we have completed our trip through hyperspace and been sailing in real space for forty seven minutes. There is a high probability the Poultinar just jumped in astern of us.*"

"That's pretty good piloting," Falon added in a thick voice. With visible effort she pulled herself back to the here and now. "Let's take a look Fred." She leaned her head back into the TCI receptacle.

"*Start full scale charging of the jump drives. Try not to take anything from our speed.*"

"*Aye, aye sir,*" Fred acknowledged.

"*Fred, were we plugged into the TCI for the entire jump?*"

"*Yes.*"

"*Great, that must be why I have a headache. Fred, insert a buffer into the interface which will disconnect us after initiating jump.*"

"*Aye, aye sir.*"

"*It is the Poultinar,*" Falon stated.

"*Twenty minutes to jump drive charge.*"

"*Falon start calculations for another jump.*"

"*Aye, aye sir.*"

"*Jason we are being hailed.*"

"*Just what I need. Okay Fred, make the imaging correct and put Walter through.*"

The star field resolved itself into the image of the Poultinar's captain. "That's some ship you've got there Jason. Not only is it fast and has accurate long range sensors but it can jump with pinpoint accuracy." Walter's eyes indicated some type of resolve and fatigue.

"What do you think I've been doing for the last four years?"

Poultinar's CO looked at something below Jason's field of vision, "Well according to the records, you've been drinking and slowly going broke." He looked up, "Then you allowed a known Imperial illegal to become your partner."

Jason looked over to see Falon make an obscene gesture in the direction of the screen. "Thank you for confirming the existence of the PsySec secret police. Look at the medical report and you will see why I had a drinking problem. It was the only way I could beat the conditioning and be a person. At least that's what the doctors said." He looked over at Falon, "Her papers are in order or she wouldn't have a valid Imperial registry code. Or at least, I would have no way of telling the difference."

"It also says here that you've been selling select pieces of secret Imperial equipment to bonded merchants and pirates. Small stuff: ghosting modules, sensor arrays, cannon, you know the simple stuff, everyone knows how to repair," the CO 's voice dripped with sarcasm. "Not exactly what I would've expected from an honorable retiree."

"Where the hell are you getting this stuff? Why are you doing this to me?" Jason yelled. "I was a decorated officer of the Imperial Navy. I served the Empire honorably and faithfully for twenty five years, thirty five if you count the schools!" Jason rose to shake his fist at the pickup. "All I did was save my squadron from an impossible situation. I saved hundreds of thousands, possibly millions of lives, inadvertently foiled a political maneuver staged by several highly placed diplomats which would have ended in the Empire illegally annexing a solar system, and for that I was forced out of the service. I honorably retired because they couldn't get any dirt on me and then they sentenced me to slow death by insanity. So don't take that high and mighty pompous tone with me, Walter Leegati. I was the one that got you into the command track. I was the one that made sure you passed the engineering parts of the exams. I have rights too and they all have been violated." The PsySec officer looked smug and satisfied at Jason's outburst "You can all got to the hells of space. Cut this connection!!"

"Connection has been severed."

"I can explain my status," Falon said quietly.

Jason exploded out of his chair, "I don't give a shit right now." He paced back and forth across the bridge. "I need a drink. I'm going below. Fred, lock all controls and systems by my voice print."

"Acknowledged and completed. Jason, analysis would suggest that is unwise at this point."

"Shut up." He turned and stomped off the bridge.

Jason slammed and banged his way to the galley. He poured himself a water glass full of bourbon, but stopped after the first swallow. The taste somehow turned his stomach.

"It's called induced fury," Jason turned to see the hairy monster sitting on one of the benches, "It is a combat technique intended to make the subject do the wrong thing in anger. I'm surprised you have encountered it so soon. Anyway, time for a special lesson to show you how to combat it and provide you a weapon." Jason was shocked into compliance. The creature showed him a variation on one of the filters, which it termed a shield. It was broad spectrum and should protect him from a wide range of telepathic assaults. Then it showed him an attack form which would render the target unconscious.

Jason woke up on the floor of the galley, the glass of bourbon sitting on the counter.

"You okay?" Falon asked from a short distance away.

Jason sat up very confused, "Yeah. I think so."

"What do you remember?" Falon was worried again.

"I remember getting real pissed and stomping down here for a drink. It tasted bad. Now I'm on the floor." He got up and examined the glass. "Did you put something in the bourbon to keep me from drinking it? I've heard about them doing that to alcoh.... heavy drinkers."

"Fred was monitoring your passage through the ship and your telepathic broadcast. Then it suddenly ended. He asked me to come look in on you." Jason remembered the shield technique. He was still doing it. He started to say he knew why, when Falon interrupted him.

"Don't say anything. Just listen." Falon took a deep breath. "I ran away from home when I was eighteen. Daddy was going to marry me off to some bigwig somewhere that was twenty years older than I. Up to that point in my life I had been spoiled rotten. Anything I wanted, I got. I had my own interstellar runabout when I was fifteen." Jason's eyes opened in shock. "Yes, we were rich and privileged. Anyway, I didn't want to get married so I ran away. I did a good job. I ended up on the bottom side of our upright society. Without identification and a codex card you don't exist, so I didn't exist. People took advantage of me in many ways. I was faced with simple choices give up and die, go back to daddy, or become a predator and fight. I chose the predator. One of my associates died, so I took her codex and paid to have it altered to my DNA. Then I started working to become legitimate. I worked hard, all of it legal. I worked my way up from dock walloper to pilot with all the licenses, certificates, and permits. But it always comes back to haunt me, that she was a prostitute with a long list of offenses and customers. Whenever someone starts digging into my past they uncover that. I think that's what they were talking about."

Jason wasn't sure he believed her, "Who was daddy and what's your real name?"

Falon looked hurt for moment, then did her sideways nod, "Hollingsworth, Robert Plantaginet Hollingsworth, he's the Chief Executive Officer of ***SPECTAR GALACTIC,*** the largest producer of space craft in the Empire. You want my name or the hook's?"

Jason was shocked, "I've had bad run ins with SG folks. They probably paid to have my Civilization treatment messed with. My reports cost them several big contracts and fines a few years ago." Jason raised an eye brow, "I can probably guess your real name. If it's all true."

"Heather Christiana Alicia Hollingsworth. Daddy called me Christy, when he wasn't so busy with business. The hook had her name changed to Quick Goodlay." Falon couldn't keep the contempt out of her voice. "She's been dead for twenty years now, but I still can't forgive her for that. God, how I get tired of the jokes and comments. I became Falon when I could afford it, but anyone digging around in my past comes up with that name."

Jason couldn't help but smile at the thought of Falon being called by that name. "It doesn't matter. I trust you. You're a good partner. We seem to complement each other fairly well. This is what Rogar was talking about. I don't care." He turned away from her, "The tone in Walter's voice and the smug look on that PsySec assholes face just...." Jason felt himself getting furious again.

"They set you up, Jason. Those guys were pushing your buttons."

"Jason, jump drives are fully charged. Do you want to review the jump course now? The Poultinar has fallen back to three hours and twenty minutes behind us." Fred's tone was carefully neutral.

"Jason," Falon got his attention, "before we go back to the bridge, I want to ask a favor." She waited for some indication.

Jason nodded, "Let's hear what it is first."

"Forget, or at least don't spread around, what I've told you about my past. I've worked my adult life getting to where I am and I don't want to start over."

"Not a problem. Let's go to the bridge and I'll take care of Fred's memory."

"Don't worry about that, I had him turn off the galley intercom when I decided to tell you."

Jason turned to start for the bridge and then turned back to Falon, "Why did you tell me about Heather, if their searches stopped at Quick Goodlay? They wouldn't have had any way to know." Jason was confused.

"Please don't use that name again." She took a deep breath and let it out slowly. "I wanted you to know the whole story. I know yours, I thought it only fair. And now that you are more in control, you will notice the way some people act towards me."

"You mean now that I'm sober."

Falon ignored his comment, "They know my past and travel the shipping lanes." She made suggestive motions down her body, "It's only going to get worst now. I was okay looking before, but now," she put her hands under her breasts and lifted them slightly, "They will think I had myself sculpted for restarting past business." Jason could only frown and nod his head. "The other part is that, last time I checked, daddy still has a big reward posted for anyone that can bring him information on me. A big reward. So if you want to make a fast buck, you could turn me in." She stood and stretched. Jason had to admit, she was the most beautiful woman he had ever seen. "My hooker benefactor, did a great deal of business on Valtair."

"This is part of what happened at the Hard Landing, isn't it."

Falon nodded, "I had spaced with that pilot during my internship. He knew me and my past."

"Okay, I don't care. I need a pilot, not a reward. First, we have to shake the Poultinar and her action group." He motioned for her to precede him to the bridge.

She stopped in front of him, turned and gave him a deep kiss. Patting his chest she said, "You'll think of something."

Back on the bridge, Jason announced, "Fred, release all systems for normal operations."

"Falon already did that Jason."

"What? How did you do that?"

"You set up several contingency overrides for me when you were...ah...Before your Civilization was removed. I used one of them." She smiled at him, "I had to agree with Fred, it was a bad time to lock everything up."

Jason shook his head, "Okay, let's review the course. Initiate TCI." The navigation plots became images in his mind's eye again as Falon briefed him about the jump.

The image showed the Boundless, several star clusters, a few hazards to navigation, and the jump terminus. A red line plotted the course straight through it all from the Boundless to the terminus. "*This is the safe course,*" Falon's voice announced. "*We can cut some corners,*" two other colored lines appeared, "*each one is risky.*" One of them turned violet, "*That's the one I recommend. It has an eighty margin, which is below safety standards for a commercial jump, but if we wait 'til the last moment to change to the course, it might throw the Poultinar off our tail. If not, the jump will take us into a known commercial jump point and we may be able to jump out before they can get ready. Perhaps with more than one reasonable jump course they won't figure it out. Fred thinks we may be able charge faster than they do.*"

"*Falon forgot to mention, that should the jump course be reported she would lose her pilot's license.*"

"*Fred, we are being pursued by an Imperial Warship and we have refused to stop when lawfully hailed. What is the penalty for that?*"

"*The ship is impounded, if they decide not to fire on it, the captain is arrested, along with the crew, and a Imperial court of inquiry is held. I see, we are already in violation of the law, so the revocation of a pilot's license is not a significant factor.*"

"*Right, add it to your programming. Falon, how long to jump point?*"

"*Two hours, fifteen minutes at current speed.*"

"*Okay set the course.* "

*"Jason we have a temperature rise in number four ion engine. It isn't above margin, but it has a steady rising trend."*

Jason's awareness automatically rotated to focus on the sensory elements of the engine. "*The sensors are showing an imbalance, but I can't get a clear picture of what's causing it. We are going to need to take it off line while I investigate. How fast will the Poultinar close when we cut speed to point two eight three of light?*"

"*Not very quickly, she's continued to fall behind. I calculate their speed at point two four five of light. They must be using everything to charge for Jump.*"

"*At current course and speed it would be five hours before they would be within weapons range,*" Fred added. "*Unless they speed up. We would be three hours and forty-five minutes from jump point.*"

"*Okay, change course and make best possible speed. Fred, put number four ion engine in standby. I will go take a look and see what's wrong. Bring Spot on line and send it aft to engineering. Power up the engineering assistant, let's call it Maintmech 3 and have it standing by with full instrumentation and diagnostics tools. Let me know the instant anything changes.*" Jason hurried from the bridge.

Jason stopped to get his tool cover-alls. As he had explained to many young engineers, the stuff they routinely worked with in engineering was deadly and invisible to the naked eye. The tool suit was their primary protection and instrumented for working with high order ion radiation. The tool suit was your friend and tailored to your specific needs and the ways you worked. He was surprised and mad as hell to find his suit had been altered by the planetoid upgrade. It was lighter, different power pack, stange instruments and had a different helmet. "Fred, they messed with my tools. See if you have the data specs for this stuff and feed it to me."

"Aye, aye Jason. I have the specs. Standby for telepathic feed."

The technical specification flooded into Jason's mind. He still wasn't very comfortable with the method, but it was definitely faster than him reading. He didn't have time to absorb all the specs, which would put him at some risk, but he did get the impression that it incorporated several of the standard tools into a skin technology, user friendly package. The helmet also had a direct TCI linkage. He put it on with some reservations. "Fred, you'd better monitor me. This tool package is not what I'm use to."

"Monitoring."

Jason fumbled with the suit trying to find adjustment straps to tighten it in some places and loosen it in others, as he moved aft to number four engine room. He couldn't find the straps, but he did think about what he wanted done to the suit and the fabric automatically adjusted to provide him with a prefect fit. It made him nervous just thinking about something and having it happen. You never knew when you were going to think about something you didn't want done, but it would happen anyway. Outside the engine room waited another surprise. Two devices hovered, both having violet auras as viewed with his new helmet. One was obviously Spot with an upgrade of some type. The other he had never seen before. "Fred, are Spot and Maintmech 3 outside engineering?"

"Yes, Jason, both report on station."

"Spot report condition."

"I am in standby mode. All systems are powered and respond within proscribed parameters. I am ready for work"

"Maintmech 3 report."

"I live by your sufferance, Varlord. Command me," The voice was rich and baritone.

"What do you do now? What happened to Maintmech 3?"

"I am an engineering assistant. I have been taught maintenance and troubleshooting techniques for this archaic vessel, as well as other engineering principles and disciplines. Maintmech 3 program resides within me."

"Stop referring to my ship as archaic."

"I abase myself before you and beg your forgiveness." The device lowered itself to the floor and tilted forward.

"Cut it out."

"Which portion VarLord," a compartment opened and a plasma torch ignited.

"Don't do anything to yourself and return to normal standby operation." The compartment closed and the device drifted back to it's previous height. "I don't have time for this discussion. Just tell me what you can do in simple terms."

"I troubleshoot and repair equipment as you direct me."

Jason thought for just a moment the asked, "Can you go and evaluate number four ion engine and tell me what's wrong with it?"

"Yes, VarLord that is within the confines of my programming."

"How long would it take?"

"Length of time will vary based on the complexity of the problem. Tighter parameters of investigation would probably bring quicker results."

"So much for the easy way." Jason turned and opened the hatch into engineering. "Follow me and start scanning for radiation leaks, anomalous energy fields and ion levels."

"Aye, aye sir," Spot responded.

"As you command VarLord,"

"He prefers aye, aye sir as responses to orders," Spot supplied.

"Truly, then I will respond as such."

Jason shook his head as his tools discussed his preferences. He made his way to the control station for number four ion drive, brought all the local diagnostics on line, reviewed all the information, then sat back in contemplation. "Maintmech 3 I will refer to you as MM3. MM3 investigate the physical alignment of the ion barrel from lens terminus to nozzle aperture."

"What is it you suspect Great One?"

"What?"

"I do not question your authority, Great One. If I know what it is you suspect is in error, I can investigate all the quicker."

"I don't want you to have any preconceived ideas. Provide me the data for interpretation after collecting it. Call me Captain not Great One."

"Aye, aye Captain." MM3 floated off with compartments opening and instruments extruding.

"Spot, insert your probe into the ion stream aft of the lens and scan the lens for deformation."

"Aye, aye sir."

Jason performed a complete diagnostic then visually inspected the primary components and known failure points for the drive. He didn't find anything to explain the problem, but he did note the beginning signs of advanced stress breakdown. He ended up sitting at the maintenance console visualizing the entire engine and it's complicated workings. The TCI allowed him to create a model of the drives from his visualization. Then he started playing what if games with its performance. The TCI gave him a speed and clarity that took his breath away. "God what a design tool," he said out loud and promptly lost himself in the design of his engines.

"*Captain,*" an image of a blond, chiseled featured man wearing a utility jump suit appeared kneeling in the middle of his model. "*Please forgive my intrusion, but I have the data you requested. Shall I insert it into the model?*"

"*What? Who are you?*"

"*I am MM3 and I have the data from my own investigation and Spot's. I have inserted my image file into your model. Forgive me for disturbing you.*" The image bowed deeply.

"*Why do you keep doing this bowing a scraping stuff?*" Jason was confused and irritated by it all. "*We are going to adjust your programming when we have time. Now insert the data into the model, then take the same data on the other engines and provide it for modeling.*" Jason watched in fascination as the parameters of the drive changed slightly as the figure vanished. Nothing appeared to change right away, so he changed the time flow to speed things up. Red highlights started appearing at several of the drive junction points as well as the lens. Jason adjusted several of the parameters trying to find a condition, which would allow the drive to function for the longest time. Then images of all the drives appeared, MM3 had inserted the data on them. All the engines had indications of rising stress levels. He played with the operational parameters on all the engines for what seemed like hours before he remembered that they had a warship chasing them.

"Bridge, engineering, what is the status?" Jason called out.

"We are on course, with the Poultinar a constant distance behind us," Falon's voice was professional. "Two hours and forty-seven minutes to jump. How's it going?"

"I'm getting tired." Jason rubbed his eyes. "The asteroid hit seems to have shifted the ion barrel slightly and then this prolonged run at top speed further stressed the junction points on number four. We are seeing the beginnings of barrel erosion. The added atomic material will increase our speed as it's swept out with the ion stream, but the engine will literally eat itself from the inside out. These are commercial grade engines not high performance models and they are all starting to show the stress. The others are holding up so far, but it's only a matter of time before they start deforming. Our planetoid benefactors seem to have been able to modify the fields and some of the outer coils, but not the basic structure. So while our performance has increased, the basics of the engines haven't. We will need an overhaul if and when we make it to port. Give me another hour to balance the engines and establish a performance margin."

"Aye, aye, bridge out."

Jason went back into the world of ion engine physics and gravitation field dynamics. He explored the changes made by the planetoid and the stresses being applied to the engines. Several ideas occurred to him about how the technology could be applied to other areas. He balanced the engine function and then created a diagnostic program to monitor the operation.

"*Jason, another warship has just jumped in not too far behind the Poultinar. It's one of the frigates. Your presence is requested on the bridge.*" Falon never missed a beat. She delivered it all as if ordering lunch.

Jason locked everything down, secured the station, sent Spot and MM3 back to their stowage bays, and then headed for the bridge. Just as he stepped through the hatch Fred announced, "Hyperspace terminus erupting aft. Another ship has appeared astern of us."

"Time to jump point?" Jason asked.

"One hour and forty minutes at current speed. The new warship is closer then the Poultinar, but she seems to be having some difficulty stabilizing. All ships appear to have increased speed."

Jason hurried over to the engineering console and brought up the models he had been working on in engineering. "Okay, Falon let's increase speed to about seventy-five percent and see if the temperature stabilizes in number four."

"Fred, you heard the Captain. Seventy-five percent thrust on number four engine."

"Aye, aye Falon. Engine is cycling normally, initiating full fuel feed, and coming up to thrust."

"Okay Fred, let's balance the thrust." Jason initiated the programs he had been working on for the engines. They all smoothed out slightly and the temperature rise on number four didn't reappear. Jason initiated the watch dog program and sat back to monitor how it worked. "Okay, let's go for ninty percent on all engines."

"Ninty percent thrust on all engines achieved. Everything seems to be normal again Jason. I'm fixed."

"One hour and ten minutes to jump, based on new speed," Falon announced. "Our friends are falling behind again."

"Okay gang, we just hold tight for jump."

They watched in growing boredom as the Boundless continued to pull away from the warships. The minutes slowly ticked by. Jason fell asleep.

"Fifteen minutes to jump," Fred announced. "Jason, sensors are picking up a strange field effect from the Poultinar. It's some type of energy field building, request human intervention."

"What?" he jerked awake, "Bring it up on the screen." Jason watched the picture build in his mind's eye as some type of electro-gravimetric field expanded out to encompass the Poultinar. Then she seemed to leap toward the Boundless, disappearing then reappearing closer, over the next few minutes easily making up a good portion of the distance they had lost.

"What the," Jason exclaimed and watched in growing dread as the Poultinar raced toward them.

"Jason, the Poultinar appears to have closed the distance with us at over the speed of light. The calculations indicated that she achieved a magnitude of light speed for several minutes."

"She will be within weapons range in twenty minutes at current speed and course," Falon announced.

"Okay, let's maintain course and speed." They watched in tense silence as they closed with the jump point and then jumped. The new circuit disconnected the thought interface just as Jason planned. He and Falon spent the hours in hyperspace making contingency plans for when they reentered real space and sleeping. Luckily, it was a long jump.

"Real space in ten seconds, five, four, three, two, one," Fred announced, then counted down. They transitioned into real space without incident. "All systems normal. Realigning navigational references," Fred announced.

"Jason, we have several ships on sensors. It appears that there are three galactic class freighters being attacked by several armed merchantman. The sensors are still not stable," Falon reported.

"Falon, stay on tactical. Fred let's plot a course to the next jump point using standard parameters."

"Aye, aye Jason. Initiating TCI."

The universe expanded into Jason's mind's eye. He quickly established the references and plotted a standard course to jump point. "*Fred, ninty percent thrust along the plotted course.*" Jason modified the basic course, as better data became available from the realigned sensors. Another globe expanded inside the image. Jason's plotted course went right into the globe and out the other side.

"*Jason,*" Falon cut in, "*I have resolved the tactical picture and it's not good. I'm laying it on your navigation picture.*" Three green oblongs representing the galactic class freighters appeared in the globe surrounded by eight red dots, the medium weight armed merchantmen, and two violet dots, the destroyer class warships. Missiles and torpedoes were being exchanged. The image zoomed in on one of the destroyers. "*They are an older Savagery class, but still constructed as a warship. Twenty ten-barrel pulse cannon for close in missile defense, anti-torpedo missiles, anti-ship missiles, and torpedoes. Both are about 200,000 tons.*" The image faded and then closed in on one merchantman. "*The merchantmen are between 100,000 tons to 700,000 tons. All have a variety of weapons and are nothing to ignore. They are about the same fire power as a frigate.*"

"*Jason, we are receiving a multi-channel distress signal from the Galactic class freighters. They are under attack by pirates and requesting assistance,*" Fred announced.

"*We should help them.*"

"*Who the pirates or the Galactics?*" Falon gave Jason a cold look. "*Come on Jason, we are only about 10,000 tons. We would surprise them but still be a casualty and give away our new tech systems.*"

"*I know, but we should do something.*"

"*Hyperspace terminus detected. A ship has entered real space a stern of us. There is an eighty-nine percent chance of it being the Poultinar. They are only five minutes outside of weapons range.*"

"*Maximum thrust,*" Jason barked. "*Shields up! Fred, prepare us for battle.*"

"*Battle stations all hands to battle stations,*" Fred announced. "*Jason, why do I have to announce that? You and Falon are the only crew.*"

"Later."

Falon jerked upright at the sound of battle stations. "I have tactical VarLord," her voice was a growl. "Initiate TCI, bring all weapons on line, put the Tigerous in standby. Their blood will be yours!" She shook herself, "*Where did that come from?*"

"*I think our unwanted benefactors did a little subconscious programming. Apparently, you are my warrior,*" Jason commented. "*Why power up the Tigerous?*"

"*The simulations I've been running indicate that we have a higher chance of success if you fight from the Boundless and I take out the Tigerous to act as a forward scout and missile picket ship.*" Falon bounded out of her chair. She stretched, showing all the well-formed muscles of her back, buttocks, and legs. She spun around to face Jason, her eyes were lit from within, "I'm on fire.

I've never felt this way before." She stared at her own hand as she made a fist, rotating it while studying it.

"Falon, get a grip on yourself. We need a plan of action." Falon started to speak as Jason held up a finger, "But it will not include firing on the Poultinar."

"We have surprise and they are already within our weapons range."

"*Jason, another hyperspace terminus has formed astern of us. We are being hailed. Another warship has appeared astern of the Poultinar.*" Fred sounded excited.

"Shit," Jason took a couple of deep breaths, "Okay, Falon go prep the Tigerous. Fred, adjust the video and put them on. It's no doubt the Poultinar. Initiate evasive maneuvering and spiral along the course I gave you."

The forward screen showed the image of a rumpled and tired Imperial commander. "Jason it's over. As we proved before jump, we are fast enough to catch you before you can jump again." Walter paused to listen to something said to him off view. "What are you doing? Your course is into that cat fight."

"Naval regulations paragraph five decimal one, investigation of and protection from piracy is the Navy's top priority. It will take precedence over all other standing orders. Paragraph two seven one decimal five B of the Commercial Shipping Codes of Conduct. 'All vessels will lend whatever assistance they can to other vessels under attack by pirates.' I will skip all the threats and penalties for not doing it. I'm going to help them somehow."

The PsySec CO stepped into the pickup range, "You don't mean to tell us that you are taking your little freighter into that fight." Jason felt pressure begin on his head. He immediately put up the filters and screen he had learned. The pressure went away.

Jason ignored him, "Walter, I'm not going to fight you, but I will lead you into a fight. Unless I'm mistaken, your orders would be to break off your pursuit of my ship and lend a hand. I'm going to hang around and see if I can help. Ya never know, they may detail one of their smaller ships to take care of us. That would be one less for you. Or I may be able to feed you tactical data after your primary antenna get burnt off."

Walter smiled, "If you weren't such a brilliant engineer, I'd say you were wasted on engineering."

"You aren't actually going to break off this pursuit?" the PsySec officer wasn't talking to Jason. "We are almost within range!"

"You bet I am. He's right about the standing order." The image faded away.

Jason pondered the scene just before it went off. He was even more convinced about PsySec's guilt. He was also sure that the PsySec CO was a telepath and Walter was not having an easy time of it.

Jason continued to make what preparations he could for battle, while keeping an eye on the Poultinar's progress. He put all back up systems on standby automatic switching, sealed the ship using the decompression bulkhead doors, and pumped the air out of the unused spaces and holds. Fires wouldn't burn without oxygen. Then he configured the engineering plant for maximum power to the deflectors and weapons array. He also found out that his battle dress had been altered as well. It did a great deal more than it did before. He didn't have time to figure any of it out.

"*Fred, extend sensors out to full range. I want everything plotted larger than five centimeters spherical. I want the best image you can provide. Scavenge computing and memory resources from wherever you want as long as it's not weapons or tactical. Ah, don't mess with the engine balancing routine either.*"

"*Okay Jason, I have it all available.*"

"*Jason,*" Falon's voice came to him through the TCI along with an image of the Poultinar, "*Something isn't right with the*

*Poultinar and the other ship is tracking straight towards us.*" Jason studied the image as Falon continued talking, "*The Poultinar started down a new course then veered back to our course, then went to another course and now they are headed back toward us. It doesn't feel right.*"

"*Fred, hail the Poultinar.*"

After just a moment the image cleared to show, a wide eyed, red faced Walter who mechanically said, "Heave to or we will blast you out of space."

"Walter, you can't be serious?"

The PsySec CO stepped into view, "Oh, I assure you, he is very serious. You're standing outside the law. If you don't heave to and surrender yourself I will order you destroyed!"

"You will?" Jason coldly asked. "Commander Walter Leegati is the Captain of the Poultinar. You're just a passenger. Hauled along to sift nightmares and ask about the crew's latest wet dreams. You wouldn't know a warship from a solar skiff. About all you'd be able to blast off is your own dick. Get out of the way and let me talk to the Captain." Jason had wanted to say that to a PsySec officer for years. Lanker's jaw dropped and he moved aside a step. He was red and shaking with anger.

"So, Walter, he pull some bull snarf order out of their file of tricks that said if a CO grew a backbone they were suppose to relieve him?"

Walter had a wry sort of smile on his face, "Yeah, that's about it Jason. He's had his PsySec officers take charge all over the ship. I wanted to go pirate hunting instead of picking on a down-on-his-luck retiree in a little freighter," Walter had raised his voice and was glaring at Commander Lanker. "A retiree with a very distinguished service record and one that had been fucked by PsySec once before."

Commander Lanker glared at Jason. Pressure started to build in Jason's head. The strange shields Jason had been taught snapped into place and Jason pushed back. "Lanker, you must be a telepath, the way you maneuvered Captain Leegati." Jason knew it was truth, but he'd bet no one on the Poultinar even suspected. That's how PsySec always stayed one step ahead. They or at least this one was a telepath. He saw the shocked look on Lanker's face. "Yeah," Jason pressed harder, "Walter's one tough son of bitch. You wouldn't get him to agree normally, you must've coerced him with your telepathic tricks."

"Full speed ahead," Commander Lanker yelled, "unmask number one missile battery. Fire when ready." He had a demonic leer on his face.

Jason leaned back into his chair and spoke past Lanker to his one time friend, "I won't put up a fight. I won't fire on your Imperial warship, Walter."

"*I will,*" came to Jason through the TCI.

"*Jason, the Tigerous has launched. Falon is accelerating at an alarming rate, all her weapon systems are on line. Deflector shields are at full power. The graviton field can't compensate for the acceleration she's exerting. Heart rate is off, breathing is labored. Jason, that kind of acceleration should kill a human.*" Fred sounded excited again.

"*Falon don't! There's no way you can hurt them.*" Jason yelled through the TCI, while he sat somber faced before Walter. A flash on the edge of the view pick up caught his eye and Lanker hit the floor like a limp rag.

A hard faced, disheveled looking Lieutenant Commander stepped into pickup range. "The ship is yours again Captain," he said. "Secondary systems are over riding and holding." Then he turned to Jason and popped to attention to render a salute, "My respects to you as well Commander McCullan. You were right, sir.

If you know how things work, you can always find ways to make them work again," he pronounced the last as an axiom. Jason struggled to bring his name to mind

Walter wasted no time, "Sound security alert. I want all PsySec officers rounded up and put to sleep in the infirmary. There's a telepath among them." He winked at Jason. "I want to know the instant they are all sleeping. Come around to my original course. We have pirates to deal with." He pointed to someone off screen, "Bring up the ThringTar, I want them to round up all their PsySec folks as well. Same treatment. I don't know what the hell is going on, but we'll sort it out later."

"*Tigerous' acceleration is within normal ranges again. Her vital signs are normal,*" Fred reported through the TCI.

Jason was trying for a name, as he stood to return the salute, "You look very familiar, but, I must apologize sir, I can't remember your name."

Walter stood and clapped the lieutenant commander on the shoulder, "Mr. McCullan," Walter supplied, "allow me to present my Executive Officer, Lieutenant Commander Lance Conner. He was the weapons officer on the Shing-Twa when you did your technology magic."

Jason remembered Lance Conner, he was a killer, good officer, good heart, a little slow on learning the ship's systems, horrible at engineering. Jason smiled as he remembered when he had told Lance about learning why things were designed to work the way they did.

"What they did was criminal, sir. I'm with the Captain, we will get to the bottom of this." Lance was deadly serious.

Jason sat down, "First, we have another battle to win. Like I said before Walter, I'll hang outside of the sphere and try to help."

Walter shook his head, "You're nuts." He glanced off screen again, "What is that thing you launched? An unmanned war drone?"

"No," Falon's voice cut in on the audio circuits, "It's a woman piloted fighter."

"It's my deep space tug," Jason added. Both Imperial officers looked shocked.

Lance stared off screen for a moment, "You've got to be kidding. That thing is doing some impressive turning and the power curve is off the scale. It took a lethal dose of gees at launch." He looked back at Jason, "Does she have weapons?"

Jason shrugged and said out loud, "She's had some modifications made to her." Jason could hear Falon laughing through the TCI at his double meaning. "You guys need to secure your ship and prep the crew's for a fight. We'll talk later. Boundless out." Jason cut the connection to the Poultinar. To Falon he sent, "*Cut the show and get back here. Don't you ever endanger,...endanger...My tug that way again!*"

"*Aye, aye sir,*" the Falon added, "*I think you under estimate what this fighter and I can do.*"

"*That may be, but I don't want THEM to know what you can do. They seem to be making some shrewd guesses based on the way you're maneuvering. We still may have a fight on our hands. So get back here and match course and speed.*" Jason busied himself with battle calculations. Another advantage to the TCI was that Falon could join in just as if she were on the bridge with him.

Jason visualized the spherical area occupied by the fight going on. "*Okay Fred, put full scan on display.*" The image expanded. As before, the three green oblongs were the galactic class freighters. Surrounding them were eight blue dots, the medium weight armed merchantman. The two violet dots were the destroyers. Missiles and torpedoes were red. There were hundreds of red dots. Teal dots started appearing, hundreds of them as well.

"*The teal items are mines,*" Falon added. "*That must've been how they got at the freighters. Fred's scan is also giving us damage on all vessels. Two of the galactic freighters are without propulsion. The other is still fully functional. Two of the pirate merchantman are cold. All ships have taken damage. I would estimate that the galactic freighters don't have much longer.*"

"*Jason,*" Fred broke in while two yellow dots appeared close to the Boundless, "*Both imperial ships have slowed.*"

"*Full sensor scans, put everything on those two ship we can. I want all engineering diagnostic routines on line. Bring Miantmech 3 to standby and plug it into the coms,*" Jason ended up shouting as he thought the orders.

"*Aye, aye sir.*" Fred responded.

"*By your command Captain,*" Miantmech's voice was very distinctive.

"*Evaluate the energy fields emanating or about to emanate from the ships on scan. I want your analysis. Also evaluate this data.*" Jason pulled up the displays from earlier when the Poultinar reached over light speed. "*I will ask for your report later.*"

"*Jason,*" Falon's voice was sharp, "*we really don't have time for scientific fascinations.*"

"*This is how we learn how to do things, take data and analyze it. I want to know how they are doing FTL. Anyway, we will be observers in this fight for about forty minutes or more. That's the outside range. They may not even fire on us.*"

"*You think it is really controllable faster than light propulsion?*"

"*Yes!*" Falon said no more as she and Jason watched and waited. All their preparations were made.

"*Jason, transmission from the Poultinar.*"

"*Okay Fred same as before, alter audio, image and put them on.*"

Walter appeared wearing all but the helmet of his battle dress. "We are about to engage. I would recommend you running for jump." Jason shook his head no. Walter went on smiling, "Since you're set on staying and trying to help, tactical recommends you change course to head straight in from here to about four light minutes out from the center of the formation and doing eggs at about ten minute periods."

Jason smiled and stood up at attention, "Request permission to join your action group Captain." He snapped a proper navy salute.

Walter returned the salute, frowned in thought, and then smiled, "I knew you were going to say that. Permission granted. Commander McCullan you are officially recalled to active duty for the duration of this action. Civilization circumvent by Imperial decree. Enter it into the logs. Boundless is now under Imperial orders. Call sign Edge, codes to follow. Deploy your assets as you see fit Commander." Jason felt a slight sensation as the rest of the Civilization programming was lifted.

"*Jason, we are receiving a complicated data stream from the Poultinar and what appears to be imperial communication key codes.*"

"Good Luck Boundless. Poultinar out." The star field returned.

"*Store the codes away, Fred. Change course as indicated.*"

"*What is doing eggs?*" Falon asked.

"*Its navy jargon for cruising an elliptical pattern from a fixed point in space. That way your range and bearing is constantly changing to a hostile. It gives them a tougher firing solution.*"

They changed course and speed to follow some distance behind the warships. Falon moved the Tigerous forward so that she was halfway between the Boundless and the ThringTar, the aft most of the two warships. The pirates seemed unaware of them for twenty minutes as they closed, but finally both destroyers and two of the remaining merchantman turned off from their attack on the freighters to close with the warships.

"Jason, strange field emanations are coming from the Imperial ships and we have received a single word in transmission from the Poultinar. Tallyho."

"Record and store. They are attacking." Jason tied into the TCI again to watch the unique fields build and surround both ships. He wasn't as startled to see the incredible burst of speed, which took the warships right into firing range of the pirates.

"*Fred, max speed on indicated course. When we reach 4 light minutes from the centroid of the battle space, initiate egg program.*"

"*Aye, aye sir.*"

"*Falon, take them as they come. Maintain your distance from Boundless. Do not close. I repeat, do not close. They will come to you.*"

"*I understand Jason. I've flown hundreds of sim hours and this very scenario four times.*"

"*This is not a simulation. This is for real. Once you get the gees you'll have an incredible adrenaline rush, endorphins will fill your system, and God only knows what else, given your modifications, but you need to stay in position. If not, you'll get my ship destroyed,*" more quietly he added, "and yourself killed."

"*I understand. Don't worry.*"

There was a shutter through the TCI, which jerked Jason's attention away from the Tigerous and back to the battle. The warships were exchanging a wide array of missiles, anti-missile missiles, anti-anti-missile missiles, torpedoes, and battle drones. The color coding was confusing. Fred kept up with them all through the TCI. Each missile was labeled with intended target, based on course, speed, and telemetry data. Jason increased his concentration. "*Fred, zoom in a little. Even the slightest event could be significant.*" The images became clearer and became more like an optical simulation feed than an actual battle scene. Jason could see actual images of the ships and weapons instead of dots and colors. Jason winced at a twinge of head pain.

The Poultinar and ThringTar started into their battle rolls slightly before the pirates. A good sign, indicating more experience in the Imperial crews. Even missiles taken out by fire, had pieces and chunks with kinetic energy which would pound into a ship's hull.

"*Why the roll?*" Falon asked.

"*Slow revolutions to unmask all ships batteries and evenly distribute damage across the entire hull, it also allows the heat to dissipate thus not warping the shield plating.*" Jason answered absently as he remembered his academy instructors and concentrated on the battle. "*This will be a battle of perseverance. They will wear each other down over a couple of hours. Finally with all missiles and torpedoes expended, near blind from loss of external pickups and antenna, they will grope around trying to get into energy weapon range.*" He recited it to himself as much as to Falon. It had been awhile since he was in battle and he'd never had a seat like this to watch from.

The ships passed quickly pounding each other in the process. Long range beam weapons were not used on the first pass. Jason noted one of the merchantmen breaking hard and turning to cut ThringTar's stern while the other pirates started concentrating their fire to cover the merchantman's turn.

"*Fred, pull out the code series and using the first sequence establish coms with ThringTar.*"

"*They are refusing to acknowledge. I am getting carrier and pulse back but no clear to transmit.*"

"*Are we being jammed?*"

*"No MynLord, the Electromagnetic emissions are not being perverted. I shall punish them for incompetence?"* A new voice had joined them.

*"Shit, they don't want to play with us. What? Hold that thought. Fred, second sequence and send to Poultinar."*

*"I can't Jason. I have been severed from control by the battle computer."*

"What battle computer?"

*"I serve as Battle Master on this archaic ship. Your simple device initiated me. MynLord, I command in battle."*

Jason was furious, "Like hell you do." He thought about all the circuits and components recently installed trying to visualize the one that would house the battle computer.

*"This one,"* Fred highlighted it for him.

Jason thought at it real hard, trying to force an override by willing it. Pushing at it just like he had with the PsySec jerk.

*"I command...I what is..."*

*"He is VarLord not MynLord,"* Maintmech 3's unique voice cut in. *"He is burning you."*

*"VarLord, I was not told. My programming...I...I...I abase myself before you."*

"Give Fred control ,then shut up." Jason's head was splitting as he spoke aloud and telepathically.

*"I have control again Jason. We have coms."*

"Poultinar, this is Boundless. Be advised, ThringTar has a merchantman getting ready to put a torpedo up her ass. She is not responding to my signal. ThringTar needs to SEED stream." To Fred he added, *"As soon as she acknowledges end transmission and change to the next sequence."*

*"What did seed stream mean?"* Falon asked.

"SEED is a small high energy mine placed into the exhaust stream. The high-energy ions of the thrust stream will mask the true nature of the particle while the SEED will actually add speed to the ship. If another ship flies through them or a weapon is fired up the ion stream, well, they go off. Probably won't destroy a ship, but it will hurt."

Jason watched to see if he could catch the speed change of the ThringTar. He didn't have to watch too closely as a trail of colored speckles appeared from her stern and her speed changed. A few moments later the merchantman turned right into the colored dust trail.

"*Jason,*" Falon interrupted, "*You've damaged your head again. You need to go to medical.*"

"What," he reached his hand up to his ear, "how do you know?" He looked at the blood on his fingers. His ears were bleeding. Then the pain hit.

"*MM3, can you generate the same healing fields as the med unit?*"

"*No Captain.*"

"*Get Spot and go to medical and disassemble the unit. Mount it on Spot then get back to the bridge.*"

"*That will take too long,*" Falon interrupted. "*Crawl down to the med unit and get in. I can monitor tactical.*"

"*VarLord, if I could recommend?*" the battle computer was greatly subdued. "*The warrior speaks partial truth. You could still command from the med unit. Thought interface works in medical.*"

"*It's right Jason, go to medical. You better have Spot help you.*"

"*I am closer Captain, allow me the honor.*" Maintmech 3 hovered nearby.

Jason got up with help and stumbled his way off the bridge toward the med unit. The third time he fell, he thought of something, "*Battle Computer, Fred has unconditional command over you. His priority over rides yours. His programming will govern yours.*"

"*As you command VarLord.*"

*"He prefers to be called Captain and the correct response to an order is aye, aye captain."*

*"Truly?"*

*"So I have been instructed."*

Jason shook his head in wonder as he stumbled the rest of the way to the med unit. His equipment was getting too lifelike for him. A gentle hiss and a prick in the arm greeted him as he relaxed into the receptacle. The humming started, the bar passed over him and relief followed. He remembered the battle computer's comment, *"Battle Computer, what did you mean by punish, and how did you propose to do it?"*

*"Send out the Battlers to shock their primitive life support systems."*

*"What is a Battler?"*

The specifications for a 200 ton battle drone flooded into Jason's mind. Every system was detailed out, every protocol, computer, power system, and weapon. He screamed at the pain in his head. The med unit injected him and hummed at him. The pain receded but didn't go away.

*"Fred, don't let the Battle Computer directly interface with Jason again."*

*"Okay Falon."*

Jason drifted in and out of awareness as he struggled to interpret the battle and fight off the pain. The battle was going about how he had anticipated, the destroyers were mauling each other while the ThringTar tried to engage the merchantman without getting too close to either pirate destroyer. Falon and Fred interrogated the battle computer leaving Jason alone. Jason dozed off after receiving another treatment from the med unit.

"Wallace, the Boundless is now serving under Imperial control." Jason woke to hear Falon's voice strained with anger.

"Heave to or be destroyed."

"What's going on?"

"VarLord, Warrior is attempting to explain to an Imperial warship, Wallace, that we are fighting the pirates. Warrior should be proceeding back to intercept station between us and the conflict."

"Fred sever communications with Wallace. Then explain to me what's going on."

"Aye, aye sir. Communications has been terminated. You fell asleep. Falon thought it was best to leave you that way so you could recover faster. She ordered us, under voice lock protocol, not to wake you. Thirty-seven minutes later two warships entered real space, aft of us and have been proceeding toward us since then. They are the IS Wallace and an unnamed scout craft of the splinter class. Falon attempted to communicate with them using a code sequence and it didn't work. Then she changed course and left her station to intercept them. They will enter weapons range in ten minutes. She is continuing to close. We are still doing eggs. Real combat is very different from the simulations, primarily in language and protocol. The battle computer is a problem. It's smarter than I am and keeps getting around my orders."

Jason couldn't believe Falon let him sleep during battle. His head did feel better so he initiated the TCI and tried to recover the battle scene. The image of colored dots and circles expanded into his mind's eye. After concentrating just a moment, the vivid images he was seeing before came back to him. Things weren't real bad yet, first he had to get control of his ship and then Wallace off his rear.

"*Jason, are you up to this?*" Falon's voice sounded concerned.

"*In a minute, MM3 proceed to space 3-7-5 and disconnect the Battle Computer from all power and force power down.*"

"*Aye, aye Captain.*"

"*VarLord, I abase myself. Please do not disconnect me during battle. I beg you. I can help you. I am already augmenting your clairvoyance to provide a clearer image of the battle. After the battle, I will erase my personality for your reprogramming. Please, let me serve you.*" It sounded pathetic as it pleaded to be left on line.

"*I can't believe the AI these things have. MM3 revised orders. Proceed to the indicated space and make preparations to disconnect the Battle Computer. Battle Computer, you will work with Fred. If he doesn't understand what you try to have done, you will educate him instead of going around him. The parameters of his programming are fundamental and not to be circumvented. Do you hear?! This is your last chance.*" Jason's head twinged with pain.

"*I hear Great Lord.*"

"*Fred,*" the med unit shot something else into Jason's body, "*open a channel to Wallace.*" The med unit hummed at him.

"*Jason, may I suggest a possible plan of action before you speak with Wallace.*"

"*Yeah, Fred, go ahead.*"

"*Subterfuge. They already know something is wrong or changed, because Poultinar and ThringTar didn't attack us. Perhaps we could pretend to be taken over by Imperial troops.*"

"*Fred, that's brilliant. How do you come up with.. Ah no. Which one?*"

The was a slight pause, "*She Raiders of Silthineon.*"

"*You cut one of my sims up,*" Falon didn't sound pleased.

"*No, just copied the tactical sections of the simulation. The game will function perfectly.*"

"*Falon, now is not the time. As a matter of fact,*" he reached into the image of the battle and circled two violet items, which quickly turned into torpedoes, "*those are your problem. They have my name on them. It appears the pirates either don't like us or the warships, because those are heading our way. Falon intercept them.*"

"*What about Wallace?*"

"*Forget the frigate. By the time you go there, it would be too late anyway. Go take out the torpedoes.*"

"*Aye, aye sir.*" Jason watched the Tigerous change course using incredible acceleration. "*Battle Computer, calculate speed, course, time of intercept and range and then provide the answers to Warrior.*" Satisfied with the answers he turned his attention back to Wallace. Jason thought about Fred's suggestion.

"*Okay Fred, now put Wallace on. Full visual, true picture.*" a screen appeared in Jason's "metal picture" of TCI showing the sweating, fatigued face of a lieutenant commander.

"Boundless, I repeat my earlier statement. Heave to or be blasted."

"Have we changed course to pull away from you? Have we offered any chase?" Jason put a great deal of anger into his questions.

The CO of the Wallace was taken back, "No, but what does..."

Jason cut him off, "Then we have heaved to you idiot! We are cutting eggs and acting as a communications picket. Now, what by all the hells of space are you doing messing with this vessel when you have a pirate encounter taking place?" Jason's head twinged with pain. He didn't know what he'd done to cause that.

The Wallace's CO's eyes bulged out for a moment and as he warmed up to an outburst, Jason cut him off again, "I apologize Captain." Jason dramatically rubbed his hand across his face, smearing a little of the blood. "It's been a rough couple of hours. Then to have to fight a ship from the med unit, well I'm a little stretched."

The Lieutenant Commander's face worked through a wide range of emotions until finally he blurted out, "Who in all the suns are you? And by what right do you speak to me this way?"

Jason kept his nonchalant manner as he struggled for names, "Ah,...Sorry again. I'm an Imperial special agent, code name VarLord, with a rank of captain. My partner's code name is Warrior, a lieutenant. We've been tracking this ship for quite a while. The Pathers want it bad. Finally, hitched a ride on the Poultinar. When we caught up with the Boundless, my partner and I had to space walk over and force a hatch, while Commander Leegeti's action group moved off to attack. I got decompressed slightly, thus the med unit." Jason waved his hand with the bloody fingers airily. "This ship is packed with technology."

"You space walked to take the Boundless while underway, that seems slightly impossible. The mass of the thruster packs alone...."

Jason swore at himself, of course it was impossible, "Well if it hadn't been for the telepaths hiding among Poultinar's PsySec contingent, we wouldn't have had to. Luckily, we took the Poultinar back from them in time and could still take this prize."

"Poultinar had a mutiny?" The Walace's CO was having trouble keeping up. "Our orders were to destroy Boundless with all aboard."

"I have secret orders which supersedes those. You will need a conformation message from Poultinar, open your combat channels and standby. You might want to go to battle stations." Through the TCI Jason sent, "*Fred, cut the connection. Establish coms with the Poultinar and let them know the Wallace and a scout have arrived. He needs to send a brief message to them confirming we are now under Imperial control and order them to enter battle.*"

"*Connection established. Message away. Poultinar sends that they are almost blind and preparing to launch fighters for cover. He requests you tell him when it is all clear.*"

"*Send back, received and understood, standby.*"

Jason studied the battle image for a moment trying to get a feel for the enemy's activities. The Poultinar was surrounded. The destroyers were on one hemisphere and two merchantmen were on the other but going the other direction. The pirates seemed to be unaware of their relative positions or not taking action yet. One of the smaller merchantmen was hanging out toward one axis perhaps doing the same as the Boundless. ThringTar was attacking the two merchantmen left to harass the surviving galactic freighter. The last of the eight merchantmen was moving toward the Poultinar. Jason noticed that Wallace had changed course to head into the fight and slowed, probably charging for FTL. The scout had turned around completely and was headed out.

"*Fred establish two different channels and standby to send this image when I tell you.*"

"*Aye, aye sir. Coms established.*"

Jason edited the image down to just the ships and mines in the immediate vicinity of the Poultinar. Marked it with relative motion, and estimated damage of each platform. "*Okay Fred, send it.*"

"*Message sent and receipt for. Jason why two channels?*"

"*So they could validate the image and know it was authentic. The probability against the enemy getting two codes at the same time is really huge.*"

Jason watched as the Poultinar put on a burst of speed to move out from between the pirates. She launched her contingent of fighters while putting her last few torpedoes toward the destroyers and then turned in behind the merchantman. The ranges were getting closer and closer as the longer range weapons were expended. Speed dropped radically on the ThringTar which caught Jason's attention. She was also showing signs of damage on the lower quadrant, forward quarter. One of the merchantmen on her was drifting.

"*Fred, open a channel to the ThringTar.*"

The image of a battle dress clad captain on a smoke filled bridge appeared. "We've taken damage been hit by something. Probably a mine," a woman's voice announced. "Damage assessment is underway. We are blind."

Jason focused on the battle scene and noted that a teal dot was very close to the front of the ThringTar. "You have a mine dead ahead. Emergency turn to port or roll to mask damaged hull."

"Hard a port! Initiate battle roll!" The captain screamed out.

Jason watched as the mine struck the ThringTar. The image of the ship's captain disappeared and lethal damage figures appeared near the image of the frigate.

"*Jason, we've lost communications with the ThringTar. There is a hype space terminus 180 degrees away from the battle.*" A swirling image superimposed itself on the three-dimensional battle sphere just in front of the image of the scout. "*Another large merchantman has entered real space. It is a very large merchant, heavily armed.*"

"*Hope it's on our side,*" Jason turned his attention back to the Poultinar and the Tigerous. Falon had stopped pursuing the torpedoes when they turned toward the Wallace and was retaking her missile defense position. The Poultinar had flanked the two merchantman and was proceeding to pound on them. If they didn't do something quick, Poultinar would destroy both of them. The galaxy class freighter had changed course and was heading away from the battle. The Wallace suddenly leaped forward at FTL speeds.

"*Jason, there is a high probability the scout has been destroyed. The heavy merchantman launched several missiles and torpedoes at the scout. The scout is venting atmosphere and tumbling.*"

The battle wasn't looking good. The pirates had two destroyers mauled but still fighting, four merchantmen, mauled but still fighting, one merchantman acting as a com picket, and a heavy merchantman in perfect shape. The Imperial forces were one destroyer, mauled and still fighting, one frigate in good shape just entering battle, and the Boundless. Not good odds.

"*VarLord, analysis indicates that the mines are cloaked to Imperial sensors.*"

*"That's how they surprised the galaxy freighters! They can't see the mines. Fred, open channels to Poultinar and Wallace and tell them about our deduction on the mines."* They watched as the Poultinar destroyed one of the merchantmen. The Wallace closed to within range and started launching everything she had at one of the pirate destroyers. Jason and the battle computer concluded that the Wallace was probably relying on surprise and the destroyers being blind and out of long range weapons to help her carry the day.

*"VarLord, analysis also indicates that we should neutralize their picket ship."*

*"I agree, but the question is how to get at it."* They discussed several possibilities, discounting most of them.

*"Jason, look at tactical,"* Falon's voice was strained.

Jason brought the tactical picture back into focus. A dozen missiles and torpedoes had been launched by the pirate picket ship at the Boundless. The heavy merchantman was closing at a very high rate and almost within estimated weapon range. *"I can't stop both, Jason. If I wait to take out the in bound missiles, then I can't get between you and the large merchant."*

*"Take out the inbound missiles. I'll think of something for the merchantman by the time she opens fire."*

*"Jason, we have missiles and torpedoes inbound from the large merchantman."* Fred was excited again.

*"Jason, what do I do?"* Falon asked again.

*"You take out the picket ship's missiles."*

*"Aye, aye sir."*

*"Fred, launch the Battlers."*

*"Only one of them is rigged for immediate launch. The other is housed in a rack in hold upper starboard four."*

*"Launch the one that's ready for launch. We don't have much time. Battle Computer take weapons control and defend this ship!"*

"*By your command, VarLord, none shall pass the wall I erect.*"

"*Okay, fine.*" Jason focused on the tactical picture again. Wallace was doing a nice job on one of the pirate destroyers, but had sustained heavy damage on her forward hemisphere and had another merchantman headed her way. The Poultinar was exchanging energy weapon fire with the remaining pirate destroyer and two of the merchantman, most of the shots missing. Another of the merchantmen was heading toward her. The ThringTar was drifting along with three of the eight original merchantmen, all systems dead. The picket merchantman was slowly heading toward the Boundless. The fleeing galactic class freighter had jumped and the other two were drifting. The large merchantman had launched a dozen or so missiles at the Boundless. Falon was lining up to engage the other in bound missiles.

"*VarLord,*" a new voice interrupted, "*command me.*"

"*Defend this ship from,*" Jason highlighted the in bound missiles from the large merchantman with his mind, "*this ship. Then do what you can to keep the ship away from us.*"

"*As you command,*" it sounded bored. Jason watched as it shot off at FTL speeds, closing the distance with the missiles at an astounding rate.

It took all Jason's will power to concentrate on the Poultinar. Either the Battler and Falon would get their missiles or not, but, either way, there wasn't anything he could do about it. The Battle Computer was the last line of defense and Jason figured it was probably better with the weapons than he would be. It knew how they all worked. He could at least be the Poultinar's and Wallace's eyes.

The Poultinar was missing five out of six shots with her cannon. So were the merchants, but they had more guns between them so the Poultinar was taking more hits. Jason narrowed the tactical image down to just the Poultinar and her immediate threat. "*Fred, establish coms with the Poultinar and send this image. Use the same procedure as last time. Keep the feeds open. I want to give her a continuous update for maneuvering.*"

"*Communication established. Image sent. Message coming in from Poultinar.*"

"*Bring it up.*"

An image of the smoke hazed bridge of the Poultinar appeared. A battle armored figure sat in the captain's chair. "Jason, what in the world are you doing here?" it was Walter's voice. "We are outnumbered and losing. Get the hell out!"

Jason frowned, "Hard to starboard, incline twenty degrees, boost slightly. The Boundless isn't in trouble yet, so I will stay to be your eyes until then. Have your weapons officer adjust the frequency of your guns. They're starting to spray." Jason couldn't see Walter shaking his head inside the battle armor, but he knew he was.

Jason watched and listened as Walter passed along his advice. The Poultinar moved out from between her attackers while improving her hit ratio to only one miss out of five shots. Jason was vaguely aware of Falon reporting on the inbound missiles and the Battle Computer destroying the two that got by her. The Battler destroyed all the missiles from the large merchant, sounding bored the whole time. Wallace was taking a pounding from a destroyer and merchantman.

"*Fred, have Styx power up to get the second Battler out of the hold. I think we are going to need it.*"

"*Jason, the Battler is ignoring my queries.*"

"*What!!! Battle Computer would you educate the Battler for me. While you're at it, educate every other AI device on this ship. Fred is in control next to me. Educate Fred as needed so that he understands, but OBEY HIM!!*"

"*As you Command, VarLord.*"

*"Jason, I have thirty-six devices powering up. Most of them are located in hold lower starboard four. They have received your direction and will comply."*

*"VarLord," the Battle Computer's voice reverberated, "We should attack."*

*"What??"*

*"We should attack. All of the enemy ships are engaged. Warrior could engage the merchant slowly approaching, while we moved forward to fire on the pirates engaged with the imperial warships. Our primary battery has a greater range then they do."*

*"We also, wouldn't stand a minute of the fire the warship's are taking. I will not risk the Boundless on a hopeless suicide mission."*

*"VarLord, they are blind. Sensors and analysis of firing patterns indicate that they can not precisely locate their targets. We could move in quickly and neutralize their long range guns before they could even fire on us. Then disable their power plants. We would be able to decisively cripple them before they could fire upon us."*

*"Jason, analysis would indicated that the Imperial warships will be destroyed before we could get the other battler out of the hold. The suggestion of the Battle Computer has some merit."*

"*Build a plan.*" Jason turned his attention back to the fight. The Battler was having its way with the large merchantman. The Battler was incredibly fast, FTL at least, which made it very hard to hit. It had no problem carving lines into the merchantman. "*Battler,*" Jason ordered, "*disable the ship. I would like to salvage as much of the weapons as possible, but take no unnecessary risks with yourself.*"

"*As you command,*" it didn't sound pressed in the slightest.

The smaller merchant picket ship was picking up speed and launching more missiles at the Boundless. Falon vaporizing their missiles, apparently, moved the Boundless up on the list of threats.

The Battle Computer provide several probable courses of action from the inbound picket ship, they were all bad news. "*Falon,*" Jason didn't like the answer, but there were no alternatives, "*Take him out.*"

"*By your command, VarLord. Ah, sorry Jason, I...ah...By the gods of space I feel alive.*" Falon's voice was filled with energy.

"*Falon, be careful. This isn't a sim.*" Jason thought of Falon in the tug going up against a merchantmen armed like a frigate and didn't like the image. "*I don't want to lose, a a a , I don't want to lose the tug.*"

"*You too Jason.*" She sent him a image of herself through the TCI. She was hard faced and steely eyed as she blew him a kiss.

"Warrior," the Battle Computer cut in with audio, "this is your attack vector and weapon spread. For the honor of the VarLord, punish them." Falon's face became stone as her eyes became death giving.

"For the HONOR OF THE VARLORD." Falon called out as her image was lost.

Jason watched in horror as the Tigerous accelerated at an incredible rate. "*Battle Computer what did you do?*"

"*I initiated battle mode in the Warrior.*"

"*Fred, explain this to me.*"

"*Standby Jason.*"

Jason focused once more on the battle scene as a way of keeping his mind off of Falon. Poultinar was venting gases, as was the destroyer fighting her. Two more of the merchantmen were dead and drifting. The Wallace was venting atmosphere and drifting. The only Imperial ships that seemed to be under their own power were the Boundless, the Poultinar, and the Tigerous. The pirate's had both destroyers, the large merchantman, one of the frigate size merchantman, and the small picket merchantman. Jason replayed the last several minutes of the battle to figure out that Wallace had run through a dense cloud of mines. Bad luck.

"*Jason, Falon has a deep seated algorithm in her mind. It causes several preprogrammed responses from her nervous system. Currently she has heightened reflex action, muscular strength, and focused neurological response. Simply stated she is programmed to kill with whatever weapon is at hand. In this case it is the Tigerous. According to the files, you also are programmed with a similar algorithm.*"

"*Falon will enter weapons range in twelve minutes.*"

"*Battle Computer, what's your plan?*" Jason demanded.

The TCI expanded out to show the complete battle space with all the combatants. A yellow arched line appeared from the Boundless moving into towards the destroyers. "*We follow this trajectory. When we reach maximum weapons range we start clearing the mines from our path.*" Little flashes showed the mines being destroyed. An X appeared, "*when we reach this point we alter course and accelerate passing down the outer edge of the most distant destroyer. As we pass by we render her long range energy weapons inoperative and cut her main power trunks.*" Red flashes showed where the energy blasts would be targeted. "*We come about smartly, still clearing mines, and do the same thing to the other destroyer. The Battler should be finished with the Large merchantman by then, as well as Warrior with her target. If not, then we intercept the small merchant with the Battler. The whole maneuver should take approximately thirty minutes.*"

"*Do it.*"

"*Aye, aye sir. Initiating course change.*" Jason could feel the Boundless rumble with the sudden thrust change. He narrowed the field of vision to just the Boundless and the fight in front of her as she came about. Firing ranges appeared to mark the ship's progression to the fight.

"*Battle Computer, you have the honor of firing the weapons.*"

"*I'm not worthy! I...I...I will not fail you VarLord.*"

"*Fred, you have navigation and close in weapons for missile protection.*"

"*Aye, aye Jason. Styx is starting to extract the other Battler.*"

"*Very well. Keep me informed as to his progress.*" Jason's attention was glued to the mines approaching them. Everything was tracking right down the line. The ship was coming up to speed as expected. He allowed his attention to wander to the Tigerous. Falon was taking her in under extreme acceleration, changing course randomly to throw off any automatic systems and destroying the missiles as she got within range. All very text-book, if you thought of the Tigerous as a fighter instead of a tug.

The minutes ticked by. "*Jason, the Battler and the large merchant astern of us have been destroyed.*"

"*How did that happen? The Battler was FTL and higher tech. Replay the sensory data and determine how it happened.*"

"*VarLord,*" the Battle Computer answered, "*The Battler sacrificed itself when it was hit. It made a high speed turn and rammed into the merchant at three times the speed of light.*"

"*How did they hit it?*"

"*Unknown, perhaps luck?*"

Jason shook his head and refocused on their path into battle. Falon engaged the merchant on schedule and started making pin-point strikes with her energy weapon. As they predicted, she didn't have any trouble cutting into the merchant. She pulled out of her first pass with a dozen missiles on her tail.

"*Deflectors firing port and starboard bow,*" Fred's calm tone pulled Jason back to the Boundless. He watched as they started methodically cleared the mines from in front of the ship.

"*Fred, anything larger than a meter gets blasted. Even if it doesn't have an energy signature.*"

*"Aye, aye Jason. Why?"*

*"There are some types of mines that are inert until they get within range. They usually don't pose a problem for war ships, but they would rip us apart."*

The Boundless continued down the planned path. At the designated point she turned sharply and headed toward the closest destroyer. The Battle Computer started firing her main battery as they closed. The weapon sliced into the destroyer like a laser through plastic. Fred continued to pick off the mines and other not so small debris that got in the way.

*"First pass complete,"* the Battle Computer reported evenly. *"Damage assessment is as predicted. The destroyer has been disabled with main power trunks severed. She is venting atmosphere and tumbling. Coming about for phase two."* The Boundless came about hard. Jason could hear the ship flexing. The deflectors were firing continuously as they passed forward of the battling warships. They also were passing fairly close to one of the galactic class freighters.

*"Fred, establish coms with Poultinar. Tell them to cease firing, we are moving within their weapon range."*

*"I get no response Jason."*

*"All their antenna must be gone. Let's make an effort to not get in their way. Fred, keep monitoring their progress. Battle Computer, commence phase two."*

*"Aye, aye Jason."*

*"By your command VarLord."*

*"Jason, the door to cargo bay lower starboard four has opened and fifteen of the mechanics housed there have exited the ship."*

*"What? Why?"*

*"They state that they are executing primal orders. No override is possible."*

*"Find out what that means? And shut that door!"*

"*Aye, aye sir. Please stand by.*"

The engines thrusted at full power, causing the ship to groan loudly followed by a rumble. "*Jason, engine temperatures are rising and stress on hull has exceeded safe operating parameters. Battle Computer initiated an emergency turn at full power. It seems that the other destroyer has become aware of us and got off an extreme range shot. We have taken a hit in hold upper starboard two. The hold appears to have been punctured but no further damage reported.*"

"*Power up and dispatch Spot to effect repairs.*"

"*Aye, aye sir.*"

Jason concentrated on the ship parameters and made an adjustment to the thrust levels, but finally had to back off the power levels. "*Battle Computer, can you start firing now?*"

"*Affirmative VarLord, but it may give away our weapon's capabilities. Slowing at this time will increase the probability of our being successfully fired upon.*"

"*I don't care. Their sensors are shot to hell and they wouldn't believe them even if they worked. This isn't a warship and it's starting to tell on the systems. The deflectors are nearing thermal limits and the hull has definitely been over stressed. Take it out as soon as possible.*"

"*I hear and obey.*" The ship suddenly slowed and temperature reading shot up on all internal power buses and the hyper spatial field generators came on line. Just as Jason was forming the question a tremendous bolt of energy erupted from the Boundless. Failures cascaded through the ship as system after system flickered, shifting to secondarys or going off line. Just before he visual image went away Jason saw the back third of the remaining destroyer explode.

"What did you do????!!!!!"

*"I fired a lens burst of DEASSER at the center of the destroyer. Slight variances cased the beam to strike the rear section of the destroyer."*

"What is a DEASSER?"

*"Destructive energy amplification by stimulated simultaneous emission of radiation, DEASSER, achieved through the controlled collapse of an electro-gravitational field. In this case, the hyper spatial fields used to push a hole into hyper space were formed and collapsed around a pulse burst from the main canon with augmentation from deflector grid forward."*

Jason blinked a few times as he tried to grasp the essence of the concept. The Boundless bucked. "Explain it all to Fred." Jason ordered Minmech 3 to reset and reinitiated the TCI, since it was the closest. Then, from sick bay, Jason's awareness expanded to encompass his ship and he started analyzing the damage done. The deflectors had been knocked off line and given where they were, the deflectors had the highest priority for getting fixed. He brought every maintenance mech on the ship up, regardless of original design, and started directing them around to affect repairs. He examined every system and established a repair priority. Their continued survival rested on his ability to get the essential defensive systems back on line before a weapon acquired them. The Boundless would not withstand even a near miss of a standard missile. The pace was fast and furious as things started moving and systems started coming back. Jason was oblivious to everything except fixing his ship. After what seemed like forever, Jason felt everything was stable enough to look beyond his ship.

*"Okay, Fred, start reporting the battle damage."*

"We have holes in several of the holds no atmosphere has been lost, a portion of the deflector array is off line, the hyperspacial field generators are out, several external antenna are missing, system resets are proceeding at a very impressive rate, deflectors are back on line, all maintenance mechanics are performing at over two hundred percent efficiency. The TCI is still down."

"*Fred, I know all that. What's that about the TCI? It can't be down, I've been accessing system data for the last however long it's been.*"

"Jason, my status data indicates that it is still down. MM3 was vectored forward to repair the deflector array. He has done so and is just now resetting the main TCI interface. The satellite units have been powered since you reinitiated the circuit."

"*What?? I don't understand. How could I have visualized the systems?*" Jason was having trouble concentrating. "*What else is going on?*"

"I have been instructed as to how the DEASSER functions. You have suffered another brain hemorrhage and are bleeding out the ear again. Your health functions are only being sporadically monitored, but trend indications are negative. The Med unit is on emergency power mode and will only be able to operate for another twenty-two point six minutes." That signaled a splitting headache for Jason. Somehow he had connected with the satellite TCI units without the main interfacing unit.

"Jason, Falon has reported that the merchantman is disabled and she is returning to support your action. She is very upset that the TCI is down. Do you wish me to reinstate communications as before?"

Jason winced as he thought of a response, "*Yeah, go ahead. Monitor all repairs and get us out to a safe distance from the destroyers. Keep all the debris away from us as before. Reduce speed if you have to, but let the deflectors clear the area ahead.*"

"Aye, aye sir. Coming about to new course."

"*Jason, are you all right? Fred said that you're bleeding internally again.*"

*"I've felt better. Battle Computer, have all the hostiles been neutralized?"*

*"Affirmative, VarLord. We were victorious. I will proceed to erase my programming now."*

*"Negative, you will continue to monitor progress until I tell you otherwise."* Jason pushed on the Battle Computer and was rewarded with failing vision. *"Falon, or .. a .... Warrior has command. Battle Computer do you understand!!??"*

*"I hear and obey."*

*"Did you copy all that Falon?"*

*"Yes Jason, but why?"*

*"The med unit is off line and I don't think I'm going to last much longer. Wait until we clear the mines before you try to dock. I may be going to sleep soon. Fred, you'd better move the med unit up the list on priority repairs."* With trembling hands Jason hit the manual injection button for painkillers. The pain was incredible, the room was fading, he felt like throwing up, and the painkillers didn't do much in the way of helping. After an eternity of drifting in and out of pain-riddled consciousness, Jason's vision cleared momentarily and the room stopped moving. He heard the familiar healing hum of the diagnostic wand passing over him, several injections were administered and then he went to sleep.

# XXXII

Jason slowly drifted back to awareness. He felt warm and cozy. He opened his eyes. The room was dark but he could see Falon, red haired again and green eyed, looking down at him. Just seeing her made him smile.

"How do you feel?" she asked quietly.

"Okay. You look great."

She smiled as a single tear ran down her cheek, "Thanks. Do you remember anything?"

Jason puzzled for a moment, then he remembered the fight, "Oh my god." He lurched as if to get up, but Falon's hands on his shoulders held him down. "What happened? Are we out of the minefield? What?" Jason's vision blurred then cleared.

"Lay still!" Falon said with quiet force.

Jason calmed down and analyzed the situation. "I hurt my head again fixing the ship, didn't I?" He could feel Falon's fear and relief.

Another tear broke lose and slowly slid down Falon's cheek. "Yeah. That you did."

Jason took a deep breath. "Okay. I'm alive now and I feel pretty good. I seem pretty weak though." He waited for Falon to nod, "Fred, am I going to live?"

"Yes Jason, you are alive again."

"Good now...What do you mean "again"?"

Falon shrugged as another tear slid down her cheek, "Your brain functions stopped once. Then came back. We thought you had died."

Jason reached out and squeezed her hand, "I'm not dead yet." He waited until she would meet his eyes and then said with more force, "I'm not dead yet."

Falon nodded then turned away. "You stay where you are and I'll bring you some food. You're pretty weak." Falon walked out.

"Fred, what is the status of the ship?"

"Which one?"

"What do you mean which one? Never mind. Tell me what happened after I blacked out." Remembering Fred's pension for detail he added, "Just the executive summary."

"You started repairs on the ship. The mechs were operating at two hundred percent efficiency when we had a near event with a mine. Post analysis indicated it was a SEED. It put several systems off line again, but using your original parameters for repair priority, I initiated repair action. We got the ship moving again with deflectors at fifty percent. Falon brought the Tigerous in close and then preceded us out if the mine area using her deflectors and weapons to clear a path. When we were clear, we heaved to and she boarded. You were in a coma by then. She was upset. The Boundless's hyperspace field generators were damaged severely, estimated fifty hours to repair and we were missing part of the field antenna. The Poultinar established communications with us at that point. They were heavily damaged, repairing that damage, and unable to offer medical assistance when requested due to the large number of their own wounded. Falon ordered me to acquire all the medical knowledge I could from Poultinar's medical computers and we salvaged the med unit from the pirate destroyer. It was installed to augment our own. You were transferred to it and we proceeded to try and repair you. While that was underway, we devised and implemented a plan for getting the Boundless underway, so that we could get you to a more complete medical facility. We spent two days modifying ships systems and structures before a system test could be initiated. At that point eight of the maintenance mechs returned from the galactic class freighter to assist in our structural efforts and three days later the galactic class freighter jumped out of the system. We were able to get underway the next day. We completed repairs while in route to the jump point. We have jumped successfully six times since then. Due to our mass and constrained structural integrity, we have to limit the duration of our jumps. We will arrive at the Altair system in two days with two more days of in system transit."

"Hold it Fred." Jason rubbed his face, "You're going way too fast. Let's go back to the mine. What kind of damage did it do?"

"It destroyed the hyperspace field antenna on the port side, punched new holes in hold port lower and upper three, severed power forward of frame one thirty-five, and took the med unit off line."

"How did we get hit?"

"The Battle Computer miscalculated our rate of turn and the ability of the recently repaired deflector array forward port side. We turned into the path of a SEED unit and could not fire upon it until it was very close. The Battle Computer provided me with one hundred percent education of its functions and parameters for battle diagnosis and decision-making algorithms then burned itself out. It felt responsible for the damage to the ship, your condition and wished to atone."

"I had ordered it not to do that."

"Falon allowed it to. She was very upset as well. They were in the midst of discussing the Battle Computer's course change when the problem arose. I agreed with her decision."

Jason sighed, "Okay. What did the Poultinar have to say?"

"I have a recorded message from Walter Legeetii for you."

"Later. I can't see very well. By the way, where am I? This doesn't look like our infirmary."

"It is now."

"What does that mean?"

"You are physically located in the extension of the Boundless."

"Fred, don't be evasive. Just tell me where I am."

"You are on the pirate destroyer," Falon stated as she walked in with a food tray. "The Boundless's hyperspace jump systems were shot to hell. So we attached the Boundless to it and took over all its functions."

"You did what!!????!!" Jason tried to get up again. His arms were too weak and his vision started blacking out as he flailed around. His headache came back.

Falon put the tray down and moved over to push him back into the receptacle. She pushed several buttons and the wand hummed across him. "Jason listen," she waited for him to look at her, "The Boundless was hurt pretty bad. You were dying. This destroyer had a section of its armor blasted away exposing the inner haul. We landed the Boundless on that section on her legs and welded the legs to the inner haul. Then we erected a connecting tube to the destroyer and a bubble over the Boundless. Next power and communication lines were attached. We took over all the command and control functions of the destroyer. It also had a better equipped medical unit." Falon shrugged and walked over to get the food tray. She pushed the diagnostic bar out of the way and set the tray on Jason's lap. "The maintenance AI's did all the work. Spot and MM3 kind of oversaw it all. Apparently, Spot was recognized as your main assistant and given special attention by our unwanted benefactors. Anyway, using the destroyer's hyperspace drive we were able to get underway in just a few days. Your shots were very precise when you disabled her. We knew just what to fix and how. Most of the crew were dead, so they didn't have enough skilled technicians to fix it quickly and the rest died when the AI's boarded."

"Do you know how unusual and unorthodox this is? The system compatibility problems? Structural integrity? Power balancing? It would have taken some kind of insane genius to think this could work. How did you come up with this idea?"

Falon smiled, "I didn't, you did. At least that's what Walter said. I told him you were dying and what you had done to save them. He remembered this scheme. Apparently, you and he had worked on a project in one of your military schools on how to best make combat repairs. Anyway, you had spouted on about how a ship could be taken and turned into a slave system. He liked the idea and had teased and toyed with it for years. So, with the extensive damage to the Boundless and the fact that they couldn't take you onboard Poultinar, it looked like the only option. He also pointed out that as soon as Poultinar could get underway they were going to have to apprehend us. So he thought it best that we leave as soon as possible."

Jason sighed, " I can't deal with this right now. Can I have some more soup, perhaps more than just this tiny cup?" Falon smiled again, lighting up the room for Jason, and left with the tray.

"So," Jason said sleepily, "why did the maintenance mechs flock to the galactic freighter?"

"Post analysis indicates that the maintenance AIs repaired the freighter and sent it back to the planetoid. Apparently, it contained a fair quantity of the minerals we had been sent to find."

Jason snuggled into the receptacle, "Great, I'll worry about it later. Wake me when the food arrives." Jason was a sleep instantly.

"As you command VarLord," Fred announced.

# *About the Author*

DT Sanders is an electrical engineer and a retired US Naval Reserve Commander. He worked for the Office of Naval Research on many things including secure computing systems. He lives in the Northwest with his wife, two daughters, three dogs, two horses, but still has time to write.

9 780595 193264